Justice Served?

By

S.M. Allfrey

This book is a work of fiction. Places, events, and situations in this story are purely fictional. Any resemblance to actual persons, living or dead, is coincidental.

© 2003 by S.M. Allfrey. All rights reserved.

No part of this book may be reproduced, stored in a retrieval system, or transmitted by any means, electronic, mechanical, photocopying, recording, or otherwise, without written permission from the author.

ISBN: 1-4140-1245-4 (e-book)
ISBN: 1-4140-1246-2 (Paperback)
ISBN: 1-4140-1247-0 (Dust Jacket)

Library of Congress Control Number: 2003097502

This book is printed on acid free paper.

Printed in the United States of America
Bloomington, IN

1stBooks - rev. 11/12/03

To those who fell,
to those who had the courage
To rise from the ashes

One of the things that we are taught as little children is to listen to adults and to respect them. That of all lessons is probably one of the hardest things to learn. Most children do just that. Listen and respect their elders. Who are the lucky ones that get the wonderful task of teaching the children? Mommy and Daddy that's who! Sons and daughters sit on their parents' knees while the lessons and wisdom pour out. There's one tiny problem though. What is a child supposed to do when the parents don't' listen to their own teachings? This will take you through the good memories, the bad ones, and the ones that a certain little boy wishes that he could do all over again.

The outcome you may not fully comprehend…then on the other hand in this day and age, you just might!

PROLOGUE

Aug 21, 1993

My journal: the wait

For some reason today it was terribly hot outside, but What would one expect in the LoneStar state of Texas. The sun was just blazing down on everything making that sweet aroma coming from the cactus flowers right outside on the other side of the wall penetrate the concrete from which it was made of. "They" don't like us to get too close to the wall. For what reason, I still don't get. The damned thing is over three stories high, how the hell do they expect someone to get over it??? Cant' really blame the guards; they're only doing their job. The job of keeping criminals (like myself) inside four-foot thick concrete barriers that's supposed to protect society. Oh well. I figure that I should continue writing in my journal since I'm about to become a part of judicial history. Thrilling huh? Too soon for my taste.

Some strange feelings are running in my mind right now. What's it going to be like? How about the feeling of complete helplessness? Who's going to do it? Guess I'll find out later on Hmmmphh!! Speaking of the devil, "they" come marching up to my luxurious accommodations, an 8X

15ft cell.   One of "them" promptly bellows out:

"D.R. CELL NUMBER FOURTY SIX OPEN NOW!!"

Couple of seconds went by and BAM, CLANK, and SCHREEEEECHHHH!!! Is all I could hear as the steel bars slid open. It's almost as bad as when a schoolteacher taking her fingernails (painted a gaudy shade of red) and running them down a chalkboard. Ewwwww!!! Kind of makes you want to wet your underwear. Waiting for "them" to enter my cell, I got up from my bed (which was already neatly made with hospital corners thank you!) and looked down to see if my shoes were tied or not, then brought my head up and started towards the opening. There were only four of "them" to escort me to (da da dah) "the building". "The building" is what all the other inmates have called it. The thing about his ominous structure is that it's an ordinary one-story (if you don't count the basement) red brick building with a few windows, a door going "IN", and a door going "OUT"...but not for all!!!

   Last night before lights out, the guy in the cell next door to me said that a humongous garage like door was located on the opposite side of the building where they take the bodies after everything is done and over with. I never knew his name because when I first arrived on death row, "they" instructed me that it's advised that you don't know anyone by their names, but by the numbers they assigned you when you were came to the prison. But wait a minute (thinking to myself), how did he know about the door?!? The regular prison inmates couldn't see that from the *courtyard. Just as if he were reading my mind, he instantly spoke:*

"I snook back there and took a gander when dey wuzn't looken. Slid by that place month. He he, kind of weird huh kid? Cheating death twice. Call me one lucky s.o.b. is what I is. Three strikes and I'z out is what dey says. Thurd time iz a charm. A bunch of stupid clichés iz awls it iz. Dis friggin hell hole iz jus' waiten to fry me. I mean you can jus' see "they" are awl like a pack of rabid dawgs runnin', and foamin at the mouth waitin' for me to give up. NO DAMNED WAY IN LIVING HELL BOY IS I GONNA GIVE UP!!"

He couldn't stop panting for awhile because he was so worked up. His heartbeat got so loud there for a minute it began to echo throughout the walls of his cell.

"Hey boy…" broke the sound of his echoing heartbeat…"name is butch."

I didn't' know how to quite answer him except with an not so ordinary:

"Brett. Brett Angelo"

As I told him my name, my hand reached between and around the bars to meet his hearty handshake. A couple of, what seemed like hours, went by before either one us said a word. Butch was the one to break the silence.

"son, jus' how ol' are ya?"

That's when I realized that he's never seen me or the other way around. I took a mirror that "they" did allow us to have in our cell and poked it out to where he could see me. All that came from his lips were a surprising:

"Damn son!! Ya jus a baby cumpar to my raggedy, decrepit old ass. Jus how ol' are ya?"

I responded: "17 years old butch."

Nothing else was said for the rest of the night, not even after lights out.

The time has come for me now. "they" usually get us death row inmates about two or three days before the blessed event(sarcasm runs in the family) actually takes place. I was told it is to prepare us. For what I'd like to know!!! It's kinda like taking out the Christmas turkey a few days in order for it to thaw in time. Total bullcrap!! Psychological bullcrap is what it is. All it does, or it's supposed to do is to give you a glance at the hand that you've basically dealt yourself. If you ask me, it's to inadvertently rub the crap in your face!!!!!

Not realizing where I was at, my eyes finally blinked a couple of times and glanced quickly to my left. Never in my lifetime did I ever see a grown *man cry...it was butch staring so sadly right at me with a steadily flowing stream of tears running down his wrinkled cheeks. Not one word or single sound came from butch. His shoulder length salt-n-pepper hair covered his face as it was buried into his hands. He walked towards me with his short and stout frame, bringing his chubby hand up to my cheek. Nothing. Nothing was heard. Our eyes met, and then broke away. Well, here it goes. Here goes nothing. On that note, the cold steel shackles (which were already on) that were put on my hands and ankles began to clink-clank on the concrete floor as we headed towards the plexi-glass door that separated death row from death itself. What a name huh? Death row.*

My, my, my...here at last, last being the KEY word. At least the wonderful glorious penal system isn't putting me back into an 8X15ft cell with steel bars. Naw they wouldn't' do a thing like that. Instead, they decided to throw me in a regular sized room with two windows (ominously covered with those lovely steel bars that weren't on the doors), a common ordinary toilet with a lid, and god forbid a comfortable sized twin bed!!! This isn't going to last for long anyways. So better not get too used to it. Who freaking cares anyways!!!!

"they" in their freshly pressed uniforms for such an occasion, removed the cuffs and shackles, then ordered me to move forward into this "luxurious suite". Can't forget to mention more damned plexi glass. I hate plexi glass.

It seems all these types of facilities are made of concrete, steel and plexi glass. The roughest, toughest, and most durable type of materials to hold the "sardines" in.

My "clear door" separates me from my exclusive bodyguard that at the moment seems to be just sitting at a desk on his happy backside chugging down stale coffee and inhaling day old donuts. That's all he does. Sits there and watches over little old me. Fabulous intellectual job…humph! Change of guard sort to speak takes place about every eight hours or so.

While I was off into another world, I didn't notice that the prison pastor inconspicuously slithered in. He was here for my "last right" and a confession if I wished. MAN! A confession. Only if he knew what he's getting himself into!

The man was here most of the night. He even ate my "last supper", no pun intended, with me. There wasn't a clock or watch that I could see so I have no idea what time it was. If there were a clock around I would be able to hear it because it was so still in the hallways of death row. Not even the tiniest of lowlife bugs were anywhere to be seen.

For the subject of supper, the word going around was that the intended "human French fry" to be, can get anything that they please. Hmmmm, sounds tempting. I asked my bodyguard if that were true and he brought out the last menu of the last lucky fellow. Sure enough it were true. Lobster flown in from Maine if you want. If you're gonna have a "last" meal you're going to make it count. That's what the guy wanted and he got it…straight off the lobster boat is what I heard. Some stupid freaking cook more and likely went to the local supermarket in the nearest town to the prison, went up to the seafood section dude that wears that dorky looking paper hat and got one of them lobster out of the tank right there. Yep, that's probably what they did. Me…I wasn't' going to be picky at all. Spaghetti and meatballs for me, garlic bread on the side. Last but not least a Caesars salad. Ohh, and we can't forget a six-pack of coke to drink. Nothing like being hyper before something like this.

Finally the pastor left, thank god!! Don't get me wrong or anything, pastors and religion of any denomination is okay w/me, I just don't like the stuff shoved down my throat sorta speak ya know. Everyone else can do what they want to, but don't push it on me!! I've got my own way of communication with big honcho upstairs…or downstairs.

Aug 22, 1993

Not much sleep was gotten last night. Grabbed a few here and there, but not much. An extremely hollow THUD-THUD THUD against the "clear" barricade is what woke me up to the let me know that breakfast was here. Harry (I named him that cause anyone that had eyes saw that he had black curly hair from head to toe) my bodyguard was holding the flat shiny metal tray filled with what simulated what was supposed to be eggs, bacon, toast, and a white lumpy pile of goo. He slid it in the slot and the food came out on my side. Cant leave out the tall icy glass of freshly squeezed orange juice. I'm taking full advantage of this arrangement of what-ever-you-want. One, two, three, your'e history as the saying goes. The feast was gone just like that! No time at all and it was gone. A shower would feel good about now. There's only one tiny problem with that though. No shower in the room. This is getting real disgusting when a person can start to smell his or her own body odor. Revolting. Dirty, grimy, putrid smell. Yuk!

Fortunately there was a shower on the opposite of my room. Harry has to escort me over there, but hey to have a clean body, I'll hold his hand and do the hopscotch with him. The down side was that he stood outside (with his back turned) of the stall.

One of the down moments had to interrupt what began as a half decent day. The prison nurse had to do a complete body physical. Hilda is what her nickname is. You think of that name and you picture a fat Swedish woman that never knew what a razor was used for. A bar of deodorant was *a forgoing word, and polyester was her most favorite material. Stomach churning. Hilda had to do everything from blood pressure to a rectal exam. A complete stranger gets the deranged pleasure of sticking her plump finger up my ass!!! She grinned while the process was taking place. On thing I can give her, she did use Vaseline. After that, the most uplifting experience yet. The prison barber had his "way" with me. Reminds me of the first time my old man too me to his barber. Boy that was friggin embarrassing to all get up. I don't quite remember how old I was just how I looked afterwards. Anyways, my "do" made me look like I had a flat top. A shiny part of my head showed thru cause they shaved a bit too close. Then my old man had to get one done just like mine…big damned deal is what I say.*

The barber got to have a lot more fun it seemed than my old man. Put it this way. I've always wondered what I'd look like bald…I just got what I wanted.

I can put one and one together and come up with a solution. This whole procedure wasn't as simple as the common person on the outside would think. Myself wont be telling you how that is. One of my last wishes was that one of the court appointed viewers that have to be in the viewing group, document the last couple hours. The lucky poor soul who has the task of watching me die.this case fry!!! Who, I really don't care who. At first I thought of the pastor that heard my confession, naw not him. I'll let the warden select. Simple enough.

The time is now. Step by step, it went like clockwork.

Prison barber shaved my head a bit more to make sure I was smooth enough. Next "THEY" told me to dress in the pair of fluorescent orange overalls that the legs came about my ankles like I was expecting high tide or something. It still didn't' sink in that my fate was soon to be death. Ohh well. What I've gone through in my short 17yrs of a so-called life, any person would totally understand the way I feel. If you don't believe me, go on…read. I thought writing this journal would help me, but it turned out the opposite. Go on…IF YOU GOT THE NERVE!!!

CHAPTER 1
"First"

MEEEOOOWW was echoing throughout the basement walls as Brett innocently put his family feline in the dryer. The button for fluff is pushed without regret. Wicked looking, a cat's face going around and round. Thump, meeeeooww, thump, meeeooww. Kinda of a tormented screeching sound. Patches of white and black SMACK! against the glass of the dryer door. If you get easily *sick when you go on a boat, this would make you toss your cookies.*

CRRREEEEEAAAAKKK goes the basement stairs as momma comes flying down the staircase.

"BRETT, WHAT THE HELL ARE YOU DOING?!? I CAN TELL YOU'RE UP TO NO GOOD CAUSE' I CAN HEAR THAT BLESSED ANIMAL SCREECHING ALL THE WAY IN THE KITCHEN!!!"

She screamed out as she yanked me away from the front of the dryer and saved the cat from delicate cycle. Hey, it was already nice and soft anyways. All the cat had to do was to go through now was to be fluffed and folded.

I had to live that down for two solid weeks…that's how long I was grounded. Thrill-thrill. There were many mischievous things that I could do from my room just as well. Serves her right to send a ten year old kid to his room. SHEESHH! at this age we're at our best.

11:26p.m. and everyone in the house is asleep. The old man's not home yet, thank God!! JERK!! That gives me at least twenty some odd minutes to order pizza...for someone else that is!! He-he-he. Not quite, let's do the entire block. Bunch of my friends and me used to do that all the time. Holidays are the best times to pull it off.

All the partiers are out getting drunk, doing drugs, and getting a piece of...well you know. My old man has another way of putting it. They wouldn't know the difference or not if a zit faced kid came to their door with ten pizza pies. They're stupid enough if they dish out the dough for it all that's for sure. This is total fun!! Just got done ordering some poor sap 12 pizzas with pineapple, anchovies, black olives, and last but not least, artichokes. Makes me want to puke.

CLICK. Keys hit the desk next to the stairs. Only God and I knew what was to come now.

Kids and parents normally get along with each other. Throw ball around in the backyard, that sorta thing. Not in this case. The whole concept of the sanctity hood of parenthood was about to change for Brett.

"BOY!!! YOU HERE???"

The old man spurted out as he tried endlessly to walk up the stairs without falling flat on his face. By the way he came in the house and the way he was acting, at least a six-pack was his company this evening. Dragging his feet, slobber dripping from the corner of his mouth, and the foul stench of cheap beer on his work clothes. Typical drunken jerk!! "typical" isn't the right word for him.

When I heard the old man speak, all that my body could do was to immediately go into fetal position and pray to God he wouldn't' step into my room.

RIGHT!! This is the only thing on that mans mind. Get up to his boys room, take care of business, and then get out. Simple as pie to him. No one would ever know. No one would care what he does, or what I think. Cause I'm the man of this here castle; I bring home the damned bacon. So I can do as I damned well please!! To hell with anyone who thinks different. The only thing that he has to make sure of is that his dear wifey is dead asleep, the other boys' room door is closed, then he's home free.

But he DID come in my room. He didn't' have his shoes on or keys in his pocket (they make too much noise). This way it's easier for him to slither in.

(whispering)

"heyyy boy, you sleep? Humph, sure ya are boy."

This hairy, disgusting smelling man begins to remove his work pants(which are soaked with oil and some other weird looking crusty crap), his sweaty shirt next, last…his boxer shorts.

(Yeah, you heard right, his boxer shorts. Underwear, draws, or whatever you want to call them)

Old man slowly pulls back the blanket that's covering me and stops.

Justice Served?

Similar to a hunter stalking it's prey. It sits there and studies their victim before finishing out its fate. That's what's different, what's so complex about human beings. Four legged animals they hunt, stalk, and kill. Over within minutes! Not this human animal. He's quite unique. He doesn't take a gun or some other type of weapon and kill his intended…eh, no he doesn't do that. He makes the torment last as long as he pleases. You see torture is his favorite game.

"Boy…"

He calmly utters…"member long time back ya once asked me about life and birds, something like that anyways… s**t (beeeellllchhh) anyways boy, ya about to learn lesson number one."

Scary things go bump in the night as the old saying goes. The boy didn't comprehend why this "lesson" was taught the way it was. Not knowing any better, he did nothing. Absolutely nothing...except for what he learned in a previous "lesson"... which was to listen to his elders.

Sort of ironic huh? One of life's lessons basically slapping the innocent one if their face.

12:34a.m. the old man finally fell asleep. My eyes were WIDE open. They stayed that way until the sun came up, watching and making sure the hunter didn't' come back for more.

CHAPTER 2
"Typical day"

Thank God it was Saturday. Everyone in the Angelo household slept in, all accept the little boy named Michael. According to him, he goes by the nickname "mikie", NOT Michael!

Momma and the old man were both side by side, covered by a quilt that looked like it was made by a grandma or something. Multi-colored patches, different types of material. No doubt *that each one could tell a story. Brett was all by himself, STILL in a fetal position. The younger boy "mikie" was glued to the downstairs boob-tube watching cartoons. Bugs bunny was his favorite.*

More about 8:21am or so Brett did come racing down the stairs like a bat out of hell, already in a pair of sweats, tennis shoes that were completely worn out in the sole to where his foot hit the rubber beneath the material, a T-shirt that had it's own ventilation system in the right armpit seam, and a San Francisco 49er's corduroy football cap. It was now time (like every Saturday) for the boys in the neighborhood to have their weekly game of dodge ball.

It's been like that here in Clover since I can remember. Where the heck is clover? I didn't know exactly where until the other day in geography class cause the teacher gave us a test (I hate test!!) and I got it wrong! She made a big deal out of nothing. There was an enormous (looked that up in a dictionary) red "X" over that question. The whole class laughed their heads off when they found out that I didn't know where I lived. Hey, all I know is that it's in the state of Texas, in the smack dab middle of desert country, and is hot as the tamales they serve at the local restaurant. Sweat pours off your forehead with no problem at all. A person has only one thing they have to worry about when they come to Clover. You cant' go to the bathroom or leave your blinds up at night without your next door neighbor telling the local old ladies gathering group what happened over a cup of coffee the next morning. Tumbleweeds make their way down the streets during a windstorm and over on Sanders St. (snob street to us people that don't have a million dollar car or call their kids names like "buffy" or "muffy") they're cleaning up the tumbleweeds cause it messes up the look of their house. Go figure. How could a person be happy with so much money? What would they do with it? An idea comes to my mind. I'm going to be late if I don't stop lollie-gagging around and get to the game.

    YEP!! They're all here. In all there was approximately four kids. Actually five, if you count Denton the buck toothed kid who always sits near the fence (that surrounded the playground area) and stared at all the other boys while they slammed a rubber sphere against each other's bodies. Don't' know how old he is either, no one else knew either. If it were a toss up, I 'd guess somewhere around my age, ten or eleven. Oh well.

Jordan is a nice kid. The only thing I still don't' understand about him is why he always wears that funky looking beanie thing on his head. He said it was called a Yamika (or something like that). You see, he's Jewish. I don't know much about it. Once (after I met Jordan that is), I asked my momma what were Jewish people like. She told me (this was one time she WASN'T drinking) that Judaism is a complicated religion, like any other religion. If I had any questions I should ask Jordan's father. I should do it in a polite way not to offend them. Momma didn't' know that much about the Jewish religion…any religion for that matter.

I did just that too. Jordan's father was happy to tell anything that I wanted to know, even if they were stupid questions. He told anything and everything. Even though he knew that I was raised being catholic. Crazy isn't it? At this age any kid has plenty of questions about life in general. School, puberty, religion, sex, they'll drop the bomb sooner or later. It's every parent's nightmare. Every adult gets red in the face trying to "politically" correctly explain these things so the children will understand. Some do, then some don't'. The ones that do understand will graduate from high school, stay a virgin till they get married, and end up having a high paying job when they're adults.

Justice Served?

The ones that DON'T understand and say "screw you" to the whole world, end up in juvenile before the age of 13, drop out of school by grade eight, (if you're a girl) get pregnant before turning 14, and end up on welfare because they've just been too damned lazy to take any responsibilities for their actions.

Here's a good one. Dick, his parents must have been stone cold drunk or slamming their heads up against a brick wall when they named him. Naming a kid "dick" is cruel. Absolutely hilarious!! What's in his backpack? The entire group wanted to know. He would never tell us. Kind of kept it to himself. Knowing that every person has something to "hide", it wasn't pushed in my case. We all had a sort of a nasty nickname for "dick" when we were mad him.

"HEY! YO DICKKKKKKYYYYY!! HICKORY DICKORY DOCK!!" The heckling wouldn't stop for what it seemed like hours after the teasing frenzies. Ti would either go straight through one ear and out the other or he'd join along in the fun. "Dicky" joined in mostly.

What goes around comes around is what dick thought silently to him.

Right at that moment, Henry slammed the ball SMACK!! In the back of my head. STUPID IDIOT!! This kid is an eleven year old that's approximately 5ft tall!! Must have been born from giants or Bigfoot creatures. Can you imagine being that tall at that age? No way! Tall jokes were never told about HIM that's for sure. 5ft is pretty damned tall when you think about it. Not one of us thought of him as a Bigfoot or *freak. No way Jose. Whenever there was neighborhood challenge against another, he would always be tending the goal area. And why wouldn't at his height.*

Once this other kid from the "other" neighborhood had the nerve to call him "two tall Jones" and all Henry had to do was to stare him down like a rabid dog gone bezerk. Poor fool wet his pants and had to run home to mommy for a change of clothes. None of us ever saw him again! Henry took it as no big deal and shrugged his shoulders saying, "oh well…"

"are ya all ready or not?" I yelled to the guys as I tried to spin the ball on my finger like a basketball. Magic Johnson I'm not…

"What's crawling up your butt Brett?" they guys yelled.

Boy, can they come up with some of the most disgusting metaphors to say or what?

Peering at them like he was ready to pounce them on the spot, Brett coldly replied back…

"Don't even go there! Ya all are like a couple of grandmas' waiting to cross the road or something. Hurry up and make ya alls minds up to if you're gonna play or not!!!!"

The guys looked at one another and knew that something was wrong. None of them asked what it was, but just continued to play. Play until the sun went down.

After while when everyone else had made their tracks home, I was at the bottom of my houses' front steps. Did I really care? Sure didn't. Sounds cold don't it? Hey, you got to understand the situation. A mother *that drinks herself till she passes out and a father that comes home (should actually say slithers home) whenever he pleases. That's if the medical field can call this two legged, brainless, no heart creature a father. You use that word out of respect for your parent, that's why I call my father "old man", no respect for him.*

Believe it or not there is a bright spot in the horizon. "Mikie". Innocent little brother "mikie". Being the older brother I've tried to "shield" him from all that I could. You see, he's only four years old and loves cartoons. Any type of cartoon he'll watch, but the rabbit rules. "Mikie" never tells or leads us on that he's up in the morning (which is usually around 6am). He'd go downstairs, fix his peanut butter and cheese sandwich, and plop down in front of the tube and watch until someone else decided to get up. Needless to say it was always me. Not in my lifetime will he know what goes on in this house!! He's only a small kid and don't pay much attention to other stuff then cartoons and toys.

Children are our future unless tarnished by the present!

Today was Friday and it was beans-n-wiener night. Being a ten-year-old kid and the duty of cooking fully on my shoulders, what do you expect a ten-course meal…don't think so? Nice and simple for mikie and I. Most likely it was nothing frozen or had more than one step to it. The can opener is the chief in this kitchen. Tin cans, boxes being ripped open, uh huh, that's it. Mom was real simple to cook for. All that I had to do was open the cabinet under the kitchen sink (which was fully stocked w/sick packs and bottles of other brown tea looking like liquid) and open one up. To me it looked very much like ice tea in the clear glass bottles. We all know it wasn't ice tea. I had an idea once to taste one of the "teas" and it completely burned my throat. My stomach lit up when it hit bottom. YUK!!! One time is all it takes for stupidity like that.

The seal around the cap was always a real booger to open, so I snatched a butter knife from the silverware drawer, slid the blade around (underneath too) the paper seal, and then took the tea upstairs. I was told to leave it outside the door and clean up the empty ones.

There always seemed to be 3-4 bottles empty waiting for me. I had to tell mikie one time not to play w/them *because they could easily shatter and slice off a finger or something on a ragged edge of glass.*

Can you picture that? A three or four year old little kid has nothing to do…he's bored to death. Where is everyone? He's thinking: "got to go find something to do" right? They're always around the house so they'd have to be safe right? Sort of looks like one of them tube thingies that has all different colored pieces of plastic at the end. Let's take a look. Heeeeyyy, pretty weird. Uh oh I dropped the bottle.

The "tea" bottle shatters completely into a million pieces right smack at the foot of his feet. All but for the neck of the bottle stayed intact with the jagged edge pointing all around. What is he going to now? Somehow he's got to clean all this up. Trying to

Justice Served?

pick up the endless pieces of glass, one of the jagged edges invited him to reach out and touch it.

"Come on kid, touch me, come on, I'm your friend" a kids worst nightmare is to in slow motion watch one of his limbs involuntarily taken away from him. Like plastic wrap you stick on leftovers, the first layer of skin has that rippling shredded sound when it's being sliced into. You cant' quite forget the liquid aspect of it. Blood people, BLOOD!! The thick red liquid spurts out of the artery, slowly dripping down his arm. Some time after the disfigurement, the liquid starts to get crusted over on the wound like dried up stale chocolate syrup. Cant' forget the smell either. Reminds me of ammonia.

It's the worst nightmare, just pray that it's the only one he ever has. All *sorts of nightmares that he hasn't experienced yet, and I pray to God that he doesn't have to either!*

CHAPTER 3
"The trip"

HOORAY!! YEHAWWWW, NO MORE SCHOOL, NO MORE BOOKS, NO MORE TEACHERS DIRTY LOOKS!!

Summer vacation is every kid's escape from education or ANYTHING remotely to do with learning. Yes. Fun, fun, fun, and lots more fun. Brett can't wait till he can go down to the lake and dig up them big fat slimy worms that he'd use for fishing. Bass *fish like those type of worms more than any other fish in the lake.*

Normally each summer about two weeks after school has been let out, the "MEN" of the family goes to the lake. It's the one thing the old man tries to do. Old man loves fishing too. He'll leave everything else behind. The beer, the late work hours, even the other women (us kids weren't totally blind on what was going on) all in the name for outdoors. There was something else about the summer time that he loved. I didn't understand why. Mikie and me always had fun at the lake and didn't pay much attention to the old man.

Brett and mikie were free to roam, up to the point of the fence that surrounded the campground. Shoot, half the time they'd climb over it and explore what was over the horizon.

Justice Served?

Only if the horizon was a small hill that consisted of the dam that held the water in the lake back. Ingenious engineering by the local beavers don't you think? Beavers take days even weeks to construct the super structure. A human being wouldn't have the patience for that. Animals did it way before us human had schools and degrees to teach what one plus one was. Ironic that a four legged animal with a brain ¼ size of ours can outsmart us with something so simple.

5:45a.m. Saturday morning and the old man comes around to my room. KNOCK-KNOCK-KNOCK.

Hey boy! Time to get your ass up; it's about time to get the hell out of here. Michaels already dressed and all. Come on now!!!

He didn't even give the poor kid a chance to answer; he just slammed down the hallway. What a royal son of a b****h!!! Why in hell call someone "boy"? he has a name! Makes him sound like a piece of meat off the chopping block or a slave back in the slavery days when their "masters" called their slaves "hey you". It's stupid, moronic, and humanly degrading. Sorry excuse for a father is there ever was one.

At last, we're here! The old man even got the same spot as last year. I'd figure cause it's right next to the lake. All in all, there's about ten or so cabins in the entire campground. There's about a boat's length (10-15ft) between each cabin with what I think are pine trees. The limbs have those prickly, rough to the touch, green sharp "needle" like objects

Justice Served?

poking out. So they're pine trees in my book.

What's funny as all get up is how grown men act when they get into this kind of environment. They start to sport cheap funky animal skin hats like Davey Crockett with his coon hat. Ah shoot, these idiots think they're dressing "down to earth" and "macho" like. This dude last year came wearing such a hat. I questioned him on where he got it and he replied by saying that he killed it. What he didn't know was when he turned around to walk away, the price tag fell out from the back of the rim. I fell on my butt laughing is what I did.

Around lunchtime, mikie got back from his great fishing expedition in a wading pool of a lake. Where's the old man? Oh I forgot. On the first day that we arrive at the lake, he usually goes up to the supply hut (which is really a convenient store made to look like a log cabin on the outside) to fill up our cooler and flirt with the cashier. Girls of any kind to me are gross. I'm just not into girls yet that's all. YUK, PUKE, MAKE ME GAG!! This year I made it to junior high, not into girls.

Wonder if my "secret compartment" is still here. On that note, I trailed my way up to our cabin. Slowly but surely made my way up the rickety stairs and reached for the door. Damn! Not budging. This is great. The friggin door is jammed and we can't get in. There's one puny thing that's good about this whole situation; our facilities aren't inside. It's in the form of an out-house by the supply "hut". Jimmie Christmas thanks for that.

Trying over and over the door wouldn't move an inch. Need more muscle behind it. Guess I'll have to wait for the old man. Almost as if he were reading my mind, here he came, with ice chest full underneath his arm. Of course he was hoofing up the path ticked off to the world.

This man would be ticked off even if there were three naked women standing in front of him offering their bodies to him. The women had to go to him, not the other way around. There could be dinner waiting for him on the table and a gorgeous blonde wearing a French maids uniform ready and willing for ANYTHING... and THAT wouldn't even please him.

Instantly the man threw the chest down and started to question the frustrated boy as if it were a police interrogation. A humungous burst of laughter spilled out.

"What's wrong boy??? Not enough b**lls behind it. Thought so. COME ON BOY, YA WEAKLING. Take your upper body; take a few steps back and BAM!! Ram yourself into the door"

This particular "lesson" lasted almost close to an hour him showing me how it was supposed to be done. Like a typical macho, egotistical, asshole of a man, he landed flat on his brains, his ass!! I could almost smell the anger flowing out from his ears.

The boy about faced towards the stubborn door and started to walk to it, mocking his fathers so called manhood. It ever so slowly creaked open.

Justice Served?

"Great this is all I need. Now he's going to be a pain the rest of the day. Better go get the ice chest before that end up all over the ground".

Some time after sun down (around seven or so) I tackled the dinner dishes. Real thrilling to do dishes from a water spigot outside the cabin. Cold water no less. Old man do the dishes?? That's really hilarious. Like everything else in this family, it was my responsibility to take care of it. The dishes, cleaning, and mikie too, all of it was for me to do. NOW is the time for bed. Bed was a pair of wooden log bunk beds on one side of the room, which was divided by a curtain, then on the other side a cot. Mikie and I slept on the bunk beds and the old man got the cot.

Have you ever heard the saying: "when the cat's away, the mouse will play"? This isn't a mouse though; this is a BEAST!

Mikie is sort of difficult to get to fall to sleep. Typical seven-year-old kid, He likes bedtime stories, puppet shows with socks, anything and everything he could think of for the excuse to stay awake. One, two, three strikes and he's out for the count. WHEW, he's out for the count. Hope I can get some winks tonight.

It's kind of chilly, both outside and INSIDE the cabin. Cause of what happened in my bedroom awhile back, now I have the tendency to sleep with a pair of pants on. They have to have either a zipper or button fly. Safety or paranoia, call it whatever you want.

Beasts love to roam, and they relish the darkness. For the darkness is their companion…their only one!

Justice Served?

Did it for the past three years and I'll do it tonight again. He'll come no matter what. He never stops, just like a broken record. Over, over, and over again…nothing will ever make it stop. I just wish something would.

At last did I comprehend why the old man loved summers. Cruel twist of fate if there ever was one.

Yeah Brett, it's cruel and ironic. Sad that a person your age has to grow up and grow up too soon. Your'e practically a baby starting to understand the large complex puzzle of adolescents. What's worse about the entire thing is that you're being steered in the wrong direction. By the WRONG one that's for damned sure!!

I wore my pants this night too.

CHAPTER 4
"Departure"

    The old man did happen to catch some fish this time. They were a type of fish that had a huge head with long, stringy things coming out of their "faces". Who gives a flying flip what they're called. They're ugly, slimy and totally revolting. A funny thing about fish is that their mouths look like them tiny plastic lick-em-stick-em things that hang witless looking stuffed animals in the back window of a car. "Baby on board" signs are most common with mothers. Anyways, it didn't take hardly any time at all to get home this trip. For a weird reason the old man was in a real hurry. I can't remember where I heard that term "old man", but it fits him just fine.

By the time we reached the driveway, cats and dogs were coming down in packs. In another words, it was pouring down rain. Might as well call it a hurricane!! I told Mikie to slip his raincoat on and haul it to the front door.

"okay Brett...heyyyy Brettttttt" (his fingers were fumbling around with the buttons)

"Awww man, du stooppid ting wont work!"

Sniveling took over him by the time I got back there to him. Leaning over the back of the front seat, I calmly buttoned his raincoat. I reassured him:

"There ya go guy. When yaw open the door, run as fast as you can, but be really, really careful ok?"

"Uh huh…"

And off he went.

He shook his head and CLICK, SLAM goes the car door and before too long, he was inside the house safe and sound. Old man didn't even wait for us kids, by this time, he's already in the house sitting down with boob tube on and slugging down a beer. He doesn't give rats behind. On that note, it was my turn to fair the wonderful weather we were having. I only had on a sweatshirt to cover me, not much to keep me dry. Here's goes my turn to get soaked.

Justice Served?

When you're right, you're right!!! The old man was sitting down glued to the TV. It figures as much. Hey! I got to get out of this soaking shirt or I'll catch a cold. There's a major test in English class tomorrow and I don't want to miss it. Hold on a second. Something isn't right here. Besides the couch potato that is sucking down a beer for his dinner and Mikie in his room making skyscrapers out of legos, something isn't quite right. Throwing down the towel on the floor I was using the dry my hair, I figured it out. Mom, she's nowhere to be found.

Not even realizing that I was saying that out loud, I went to look for her. Wonder where she could be. Momma's not in "her" room. Not in the bathroom either. When I got to the kitchen and looked in the garbage can for the leftovers of empty "tea" bottles, there wasn't any garbage for that matter. Now THAT'S confusing.

More confusing than you think boy, more than you know!!

Doing something that really didn't agree with me, I turned to the old man and questioned him.

"Hey, where's mom? She's not in her room or the house for that matter."

All the fat slob could do was to take another sip of beer, let out a disgusting loud burp, and crush the can after he was done.

Anything would help at the moment. This is going to get nasty if he doesn't tell me where she is. The old man at last finally looked at me and coldly said:

"Stupid b***h is gone, she's been gone since after we left for the lake.

Justice Served?

Drinking herself slapping drunk and screwing every tom dick and Harry in this friggin town is all she did. And you know what boy?"

How ice hearted can a father get? This person might as well have an iceberg in the hole where his heart is. Or where it'supposed to be.

Shrugging my shoulders to this "thing" as a line of tears began to run down my cheek is all that I could do.

(BEELLLLCCHHH) "...don't give a flying s**t either! She wasn't worth a pot to pee in. That's it, she was a pot and I'd be the one taking the p*ss. Slut! Don't get all teary eyed on me now. Aint worth it."

Old man glances over to Brett and sneers.

Without mom here what are we going to do? Thought as a steadier stream of tears flooded him. Mikie isn't going to understand mom leaving. For what reason, I still don't know. I swear to God that I will find out!! Listen you sorry worthless piece of human, drunk lump of lard, you better tell me where she is and tell me the REAL reason momma left or I'll shove that blessed aluminum can down your fat dirty throat!!! So fess up old man…WHERE'D SHE GO???? As least that's what I wanted to do.

If I said anything remotely, anything that came close to talking back, my teeth wouldn't be in my mouth anymore. Either that or, well you know. I'd take missing teeth over that any day of the week.

"Boy, get me another brewski (blawwwruuuup) and toss this one in the trash."

And he handed me yet ANOTHER useless can.

You see this old man? The can which was now in my left hand. I took it and quickly crushed it in between both hands and brought the demolished "container" up above his head (standing right behind him) with the intention of doing some major damage with it.

Almost as if he knew something was going down, the "old man" briskly did a three sixty in the chair gazing up at the boy…

"Whatcha doing boy? Yeah right. You think yaw can go up against me, think sweet boy. Yaw aint strong enough to challenge me boy! See, your momma aint here now. Like she even cared aboutcha' before. A fifth of whiskey was her only child. It's only you and me…

Couldn't' make out any other words after because he was "slurring" together his words so bad. Almost to the point where he was drooling like a rabid dog being bitten by a coon, right out the corner of wrinkly stinky lips. Later yaw old man, later!!

What was to take place now? No mother anywhere around and a younger brother that doesn't have a clue about what's going on. Pure souls like his shouldn't be exposed to that type of "evil". It's probably for the better that he was so naïve. Maybe the old man said something truthful for once. "A fifth of whiskey is her only child". Her being in the condition that she was in, it was for the better. The women had TWO sons though. Not a thing will happen to him and Brett will make sure of that it if it takes every ounce of his body and soul.

Justice Served?

Speaking of the devil, guess I'd better look for him. Old man doesn't plan to go anywhere soon. Let's see, he's either in his room or the backyard. Sometimes Mikie likes to go to his room and play G.I. Joe in a tent. The tent is really his bedspread that's supposed to be on his bed!

"BANG!! BANG! aw wight joe, get da bad guys."

Exactly what I thought he'd be doing. The bedspread was hanging over the end board and was draped to the dresser a couple feet away. Can't forget the door (one of my plaid shirts) that was son it's way to falling off the roof of the tent.

"AW MANNN!! STOOPIT THINGIE, STAY UP DER!! Heyyy Brett, whatcha doing here?? Wanna play Joe wit me? Huh? Huh? Come on, pleeeeeeasssssseee pway wit me."

The" door" of the tent did fall on the floor and my fixit came to the rescue. While Mr. Goodwrench was putting the door back up on military headquarters, things or actually, WAYS of telling the younger brother that his drunken mommy up and decided that she didn't want him no more completely engulfed his mind. Kids were only in the way in the world according to booze. She found happiness elsewhere. besides with him. He's not old enough to comprehend what his older brother has to tell him. To Brett, who'd want to be in his shoes?? Anyone with a sane mind wouldn't!!

Brett sat down on the floor, folded his legs Indian style, took a single deep breath, and flipped back his bangs from his forehead and looked up at his little brother.

Justice Served?

"mikie, come on over here for a sec okay?"

Mikie poked his head out from under his bed (foxhole in military terms) and boyishly replied:

"Whatcha want Brett? Did I boo-boo or sumpin bad? I ditunt put no shooger in da sawlt shaker, uh uh, no way Jose!! Nawt me, so whatcha want?"

The messenger had to deliver the news and then mend the wounds later.

"Momma's not here anymore Mikie. She isn't coming back either."

At least that's what I got from the old man; she's not coming back.

Continuing: "yaw going to have to be strong now okay guy? Momma had to go take care of herself."

Why am I kidding myself?? The boy has some intelligence for his age.

Seven-year-old kids are a lot smarter then we give them. Geniuses in a size four shoe! They read books like "cat in the hat" and other kiddie stories. It wouldn't surprise me none if he was reading encyclopedia's and dictionaries when no one is looking. One thing that momma did give him last year for Christmas was a kiddie dictionary with pictures that would explain the words clearer for people his age. Wonder if he does try to read it? Oh well, big bro is going to have to help him now. Even though old man is still here (in a physical sense) I'll become his "daddy" now.

Mikie didn't even sniffle or shed a tear.

"Brett, momma…"

His tiny head tipped downwards looking at his shoes, then back up again to me.

"...gone away cuz of da bawown tinky boozie huh? Dat stuff made momma a meaanie pants huh Brett? Whatcha tink Brett. I'm sorta happy data she's gone cuss maybe she come back all betters and bee a wheel momma. Whatcha tink bro?"

My tongue was hanging half out of my mouth (trying to reach the floor it seemed) and my eyes just stayed there WIDE OPEN as if they were spot lights of some kind. HOLY COW! this kid is smart. He had the right frame of mind though. Too bad it was wishful thinking. A type of answer had to be given to him, owe him that much.

"Don't quite think so bro, momma's not coming back. I feel that she's gone forever. We'll be alright by ourselves guy, just you and me."

Right out of the blue he stopped me "and dada too??"

"Daddy isn't going to be much of anything with momma not being here, so we have to do things without him okay. He'll be working mostly anyways. Nothing to worry about ok dude."

"I aint Brett."

A miniature adult in a child's body going about his normal way of living, thinking freely, not a soul in the world to worry about. A child shouldn't have to worry over things like daddy not being home cause he's on an all nighter and picking up trashy loose waitresses at the local hole in the wall. Him and his brother is what count now. When I get old enough, we'll move out of this hellhole so that "IT" cant happen to him. Wont be a chance in hell for that to happen.

CHAPTER 5
"Nurse Tate"

The halls of junior high aren't that bad, at least as bad as I thought they would be. All kinds of people rushing to their classes almost crashing me to the floor, getting books and pencils from their lockers, then slamming then shut with a BANG! Heyyyy, wait a second. I know now what lockers are really used for. Over by my locker (unfortunately) one huddled mass of body was a pair of students (what "advanced" junior high students would call) "sucking face!!! EWWWWW, completely gross and disgusting. For crying out loud, when do they come up for air? Bet they go home with red rings around their lips and use tons of chapstick.

"Excuse me, but could I get to my locker please, I'm going to be late for English class."

I'll be dipped in doo; they do come up for air after all. The lovesick girl puppy throws in her two bits:

"My god, pointdexter here is going to be late for class, awww isn't that sweet!!"

The final warning bell rang.

"See pointdexter, now we're all late. Bet you never even seen the detention hall before. Guess what? Now ya will!! See ya there smarty pants" and she cackled as she walked away wiping the "ring" off her lips.

Nurse Tate was taking care of a gym accident involving a baseball and some poor souls face.

"Son, I'm going to have to call your mom. Whoever threw that ball, threw it hard enough to break your nose!"

Even though at the time she was giving this ducky sounding teenager bad news, her voice rang with gently, sweet sounds. This nurse you see wasn't an ordinary nurse. Not the kind that's old hair, wears glasses, and knee high stockings that went up to her knees. Nope, not this nurse. She could be a centerfold for one of them girlie magazines. I'm getting a woody just thinking about it. Calm down junior, cant walk in the nurses office with you wanting to stand up and say "hi!" to everyone in sight. Her *hair was a shiny golden blonde that would go down to her waist if it weren't up in a ponytail on top of her head. Downwards to her knockers that seemed to be almost enough for a handful. Maybe bigger. Oh yeah, her behind, her butt, her rump, whatever you want to call it. Put it this way, she's not wearing any panties right now!! Enters left stage the "sick" person…*

"Ooohhhhhh."

Nurse Tate quickly turns around and looks at the sickly person.

"What's wrong dear? You look totally out of it."

"Sorry nurse Tate, but I just got done tossing my cookies all over the bathroom floor. Must have been today's mystery meat surprise or something…"

Justice Served?

Hook line and sinker!! She hands me a hall pass, scribbled something on it, and tells me:

"Go on home cutie pie, but make sure you show this to the attendance office in the morning for your entry slip back into school okay? Hope you get better dear."

Those blues of hers made me melt almost like when butter does on a firing hot griddle.

Out and on my way!! Ye-hawww, ride em cowboy!! Looking down realizing something so humiliating.

Junior DID decide to say hi to everyone and nurse Tate KNEW about it too!!

CHAPTER 6

Boy am I glad that I wasn't in English class on Friday. The assignment was to make a day-to-day journal at school and we'd have to write about the topic that the teacher had up on the chalkboard. Things like "what's your favorite food?" "where do you like to go for summer vacation?", and the most recent entry(for today) "what's the most scariest thing that has happened to you?". Only if the man knew the answer to that one!!

When everyone else was done, they put their journals in the journal "box" and Mr. Webb started class. He was talking but this student wasn't totally there. There wasn't anything I could write about today. A page or so is my normal size entry, not today...it was left blank. Later on during class, Mr. Webb with his deep voice questioned me:

"Brett, how come there's nothing in your journal today?"

The only expression that came from me was that my eyebrows rose up in the "I don't know why" mode, accompanied by the shrug of the shoulders. Might as well make something up to get him off my back.

"Don't know Mr. Webb. It was too scary to put down on paper for all to

read I guess. I'll happily take an "f" for today's entry, but I can't write it down and go through that again."

He looked at me sort of puzzled and then said:

"All right Brett, it's okay. You wont have to take an "f" for today. Since you explained why, it's okay. Uh, almost end of class. I'll see you tomorrow Mr. Angelo."

"Sure Mr. Webb…tomorrow."

WHEW!! He fell for it. THANK GOD!! This gives me an idea. Instead of keeping all my feelings in about "it", I can start a journal of my own, a private journal at home that I can hide when I'm done. Hey pretty cool idea! Thanks Mr. Webb.

The bell rings and the perplexed teacher sits down at his cluttered desk. "What can I do?" Roger Webb thinks to himself. There is something *definitely tragically wrong that the boy is keeping inside, but what? Can't jump to conclusions (as he shuffles some of the papers into a neat pile). We'll see what he writes in his journal; maybe it's nothing at all. That's it; it's nothing to worry about.*

It's nothing all right concerned teacher, nothing but a thirteen-year-old boy being "toyed" with. Literally toyed with!! School is this boy's only haven away from this brute called a parent. Yes, most parents do genuinely love their children. They buy them toys at Christmas time, puts money under their pillows for when the "tooth fairy" comes. NOT this so called person. All this sorry son of a b***h parent likes to give his son a hand under his bed sheets at night!! Only if you knew dear Mr. Webb, only if you knew.

S.M. Allfrey

"Dear journal:
It all started when I was about nine or ten…"
The journal became my best and only friend I've ever had or ever will for that matter.

CHAPTER 7
"Girls"

They're all over the place like weeds, what am I to expect? I'm sort of beginning to like them now. All they do is wear those short mini blue skirts with their long pretty hair going down to their butts. GIRLS, GIRLS, GIRLS!!!! I never thought in a million years that I'd ever like them. For crying out loud I sure do now! One in particular…Marie Collins.

There was a book I read once upon a time that described a girl as a "vision of loveliness". Not until now did I know what it meant.

Marie wasn't' only a vision, she WAS loveliness. She had long straight blonde hair that would shine when the classroom light was on. Even more was when she was outside in the sunshine. Her eyes were kind of a brownish golden with a fleck like glitter pieces that sparkled when she'd look at me. Let's not talk about her body okay that would be coldhearted to "junior"!! Junior doesn't give a hoot, he'll say "hi" to her any day of the week. One itsy bitsy detail though, she doesn't know I even exist.

We'll have to fix that indiscretion now wont we? Kid has to be able to enjoy his life somewhat. Here's another one for you. He sits next to her in English class. This is going to a fun year for sure. She'll go to sit down and her skirt unknowingly rides up her thigh to where he can see a smooth tanned surface and it stops there because she pulls it back down after feeling a "draft". AW SHOOT!! Everything about this girl is completely awesome in his mind. Will he have enough gumption to do anything about his feelings? Let's see...

Pure beauty is the only word for her. If there were any other, I'd like to know it.

Today's journal topic was an easy one:

"Describe the perfect person for you and why?"

One question popped in my mind that I had to ask Mr. Webb about.

"Mr. Webb, you're the only one that looks at these aren't you?"

He oddly looked at me as if I had a huge pimple on the end of my nose and it was about to explode.

"Why yes I am Brett, you can write anything you want to in your journal. You should realize that now that you've had me for two years."

What a reality check...I HAVE had him for two years now. He can be trusted then. My entry wasn't' that long at all. The first part of it went:

"Describe the perfect person for you:

Marie Collins

"And why..."

Look at her that should be enough!!!

After being around her, I've gotten over the feeling that it was gross and disgusting to even like a person of the opposite sex. Come to think of it, a

Justice Served?

couple years ago when I saw those two in the fall glued to each others lips, I can see Marie and me like that!! Other guys around school talk about girls and the "feeling" that they get. One said it was like loosing your mind, not knowing what to do with yourself. Another described it as being a puppy that lost its mother and you'll trail behind the girl as is if she were an automobile and you're chasing it. How I describe it is actually ordinary. You'll begin to like things that you didn't before. Gushy-mush love songs, smells of perfume, lastly, wanting to get near a girl. Wanting to touch your lips to hers ever so gently. Me wanting all of my body touching hers!! Well not everything, some things I am too young for yet. I wish my father would realize that. Kissing…I could go for that.

BRINNNNNNGGGG!!! Goes the bell to end class. The anxious students were hurrying to gather their books and jackets when all of a sudden:

"Brett?"

Who the heck was that? and turned around. Marie Collins was directly in front of me. I'll take her right now in my arms and kiss her like she's never been kissed before. Make her body melt like she were an ice cube on a hot steamy sidewalk.

"Earth to Brett…hellllloooo in there."

Her luscious browns met mine. You idiot, answer the girl…

"Hey Marie, what's up?"

Justice Served?

Hurriedly she gave me a folded up piece of notebook paper that had something written on it…

*TO: Brett
From: Marie c.
(Please read right away!!!)*

This is outrageous!! By the time I read that, she was out of the classroom. Well damn it! Talk about quick! I've got to read this "right away" message. That was the last bell of the day. Cool, last class. Where can I read this and be in private? I know where, the bleachers. The place will be emptyville. There are days when I go there cause I know that mikie goes to a friends house to play. Get time to be in peace. Plus it's Sort of nice out today too. The sun was out shinning over the entire field. They were quite empty as it normally is…good. Where was that note again. Is it in my back pocket? Nope it's not there. My jacket? Uh-huh…

All right you hormonal adolescent, feel in your FRONT pockets. By George I think he's got it…

It got sort of wrinkled after being shoved into my front pocket. Here goes:

"Dear Brett:

I kind of, well, just wanted to know if you're Busy on Friday cause…well I kind of would like you to come with me to a movie. I guess I'm asking you out on a date. Weird huh? You don't have to, but I'd really like to go with you. I've got to be real crazy to ask something like this. Might as well tell you everything while I'm at it. I've *noticed YOU watching me in English class. I thought you wouldn't like me. But I really like you and would like it if we got together somehow you know. Better go now. Hope you don't think badly of me for saying this. Write back if you want to. Or even if you don't...I don't know what I'm saying. See ya later.*

M

A single "m" for her signature. Is she out of her mind??? Of course I'll go out with her. I'll also write her back too. In all my dreams would I ever believe this is happening? I'm the shyest person in the world and I've just met my match!! Marie, Marie, Marie. It's all I could think of the rest of the night. What am I going to write back? Cant come on too strong or I'll scare her away. Honesty. That's what I'll write is how I really feel.

Why me? She's never looked at me before. Or talk to me for that matter. 4:32p.m. Oh no, I've got to get home!! Old man will be home about 5:15p.m. Harrumph, like I'm real enthused. As if she were reading my mind, she rams into me like she were a Mack truck as I was stepping off the bottom step of the bleachers.

Talk bout a first impression!! Practically boldly slamming her to the concrete like two wrestlers Would on the sports channel. Thud- went her butt, crash gone all the books that she had in her hands. What a complete and total clumsy idiot!!!

"Oh crap! Are you okay Marie? My mind wasn't here and I was in a massive rush to get home. Is there something I could do for you?"

I know what I'd like to do for you!!! Kissie- kissie that's all.

He knew for sure THAT wasn't said out loud!!

Once more my eyes peered downwards to her evenly tanned thighs. Why me? This has got to be teenage puberty torture. She glanced up at me while brushing off the dirt that was on both landmarks.

"Naw, I'm fine, accidents happen. Sort of embarrassing to tell the truth…I, um, I come to the bleachers all the time cause no one's normally here and study for a few hours. Times I just sit here and daydream. What are you doing here??"

"Same thing really. Sorry bout he head on there. Sure you're okay?"

Anything…I'll kiss and make it all feel better. What can I say? I'm your common ordinary 15yr old horny teenager, well almost 15 in a few weeks.

Bluntly she replied:

"I'd be better if I knew your answer for Friday night was!!!"

As an innocent, coy looking smirk grew on her face.

If she knew what she does to me, all the feelings that I get standing next to her. One thing I do know is that I'll have to change my underwear when I wake up tomorrow morning!! Think about it…

"There's only this that I could say to you Marie Collins…"

The look on her face was as if she'd been a baby with a pacifier that was taken away so cruelly.

"…Friday night sounds good to me!! One thing though."

"What?"

"Could we not go to the movies, kind of low on funds you know…"

I didn't want to lean on of what kind of person my old man was. Not her. She shouldn't be exposed to the beast.

"Sure, that's cool!! Whatcha want to do then?"

She did not have to ask that now did she? He he he. It's like wanting to get love from somewhere I'm sure not getting any sort of affection at the home front.

"Lets figure that out in the next couple of days, it being only Monday and all…"

5:00p.m, awww damn!! Now I've really got to go, talk about hauling butt home.

"I really, really got to go…see you!!"

And started to run as fast as I could home. I couldn't even hear if she answered me at all. In her mind she did though. He would really be shocked if he could be there!

Both of us made it…and without any more body collisions. Quite a bit of sneaking glances at each other. The whole time Mr. Webb was talking, we were in the land of "teenage love". Confusing but yet enjoyable land.

Ever single person, human person with any feelings, has gone through teenage-puppy love. It's Love, lust, whatever the parents want to call it. This is the only time in this boy's life that is completely his!! No one will grossly snatch it away from him. He wont let it happen. They way he feels around her is unexplainable…yet… somehow he'll find a way to comprehend it. All he wants to do now is to soak it up and keep it there as long as he can. Love is the best

Justice Served?

thing that could have ever happened to him.

We did make it till Friday. Don't know how, but we did. Talk about two eager beavers. The old man didn't even know that something else was going on in my life. He makes it his business to know every small detail in my life. It's a morbid hobby for drunks and freaks like him. There was no way in this universe that this was going to get taken by him!!

The "plan" of getting out of the house worked better than I thought it would. You see, most Friday nights the old man slithers to any one of his floozies and doesn't care to come home until late Sunday night. Mikie goes to me-maw's house if I've got to be alone for long periods of time with him. Me-maw's knows that the old man does and realizes that a fourteen (almost 15!!) year old kid shouldn't have the sole responsibility of parenthood, so she takes him on the weekends to relieve me of "duty". Typically I have nothing to do, sit around the house, do homework, and pick up after the old man. Empty beer cans and stinky ass boxer shorts litter the floor. Them boxer shorts make me totally sick to my stomach. Kind of like when that chick in the Exorcist movie that spews lumpy green bile half way across her bedroom and splatters the wall entirely...watching it run down the panels, sticking as it went, it totally leaves Nasty taste in the back of my throat...ewwwwww!!!

6:37p.m. "IT" has arrived!! Little bro already at me-maw's and the old man didn't even grace us with his presence tonight, which means he decided to go floozie hunting immediately after work. Marie and I decided to meet at the school stadium cause of the football game. School students got in for free which is right along my budget. What the old man had no idea was that there was some cash stashed away in secret hiding for rainy days. It is going to be my brother and mine's escape from this hellhole to be precise. 6:45p.m. and the game starts at seven. School wasn't really that far away. Time to head for my "dream".

Closer and closer, and the closer he got to the stadium, the blaring sound of the band and announcements coming from the speakers…his heart might as been running a marathon it was pumping so fast. This boy could have been high on some drug and not took a care in the world. The sweat was pouring down his face, running into his eyes stinging them to the point where his hands became "windshield wipers" for his eyes. Major basket case in some people's minds. Calm down a level Brett, it doesn't get any better. Believe it or not it will get worse. She'll only make you loose your appetite next. Hahahahahahah!! Right before class let out they finally decided to meet by the stadium locker rooms. It's getting to be that time Brett. Are you ready? Have you ever had a dream come true before Brett? One's about to for you.

Part two of Ch. 7

7:15p.m. this is cutting it too close for comfort now…should've known it was a joke. Beautiful girl goes for nerdy boy as a bet between her and her girlfriends. Makes me feel like a big lump of decaying dog doo. Stupid friggin idiot to think Marie would think anything of you. Dream, a bad dream, that's all it was. Utter bull!!

"Earth to Brett…"

Only one body could belong to that voice. My dream that's who…Marie Collins.

"I didn't mean to be so late, but my dad had to stop and fill the car up cause he forgot to this morning. You're not mad are you???"

A weak spot of mine is when a girl slaps on those doggie whimpering looking eyes with pouty lips to add to it. MAN!! She drives every single pore on my body wild. Go back to sleep "junior"…down boy down…

"Nah, I'm not mad."

"Did you think I was joking when I didn't show up at first?"

She's good, pretty dang good!
"Well…" was all that came out.
"I couldn't do something so cruel like that to someone I've liked…"

S he quickly reached and grabbed my hand before I even realized what she'd said. And began walking to the bleachers. *This is it. Long at last a girl that actually likes me. What am I supposed to do is what I'd like to know.*

Take it slow Brett…take it nice and slow…

Let nature take its course I guess. All the way throughout the game, we began to talk and get to know one another even more. The extreme loudness of the fans cheers, the parents telling the ref when their kid made a touchdown, and popcorn flying in our faces, didn't phase us a bit. Pictures, flashes of her and me *were zipping in and out of my mind like wild fire in a dry desert. An answer had to be given to a question in my mind or I'll burst at the seams.*

"Marie, you never gave me the time of day before this week and now all of sudden we're out on a date that YOU asked me one. Why? By the way you acted towards me, I thought you HATED me. Curious you know."

There you go you big ignoramus piece of...can't even come up with a word to describe myself. She'll up and leave now. If she didn't hate your guts then, she will now!!

"I, um don't know how to say this Brett, but umm..."

GO TO HELL is what's coming next. Brace yourself; she's about to blow...

"I uh, have always had a crush on you since the beginning of the year and didn't know how to approach you without seeming like I was coming on too strong. The "floozie" type reputation that picks up scumbags is what I don't want!!! It was getting to me though cause we'd sit in English right next to each other and we'd be too embarrassed to say a word, when actually I wanted to get to know you better!!"

A floozie you could NEVER be. Not in this world. FINALLY it was out. Both of us felt the same way about one another. There wasn't anything in the entire world that I wanted to do besides hold her close, tell her what my thoughts were of her. What I wish would happen between us. The old man in his demented way would say:

"Yeah, go ahead and bag the slut. The younger the better!!"

No wonder momma was a drunkard and ran away from us. With that attitude and fat foul smelling slob, who in their right mind wouldn't want to get the hell away?

Hello Brett. Don't keep the young lady waiting, she'll slip right between your fingers and will no longer be your dream…

Snapping out of my daze, I finally got the nerve to answer her.

"I just thought when you didn't show up and it was getting later and later, that this whole thing was a joke on me. Now that you've said how you feel…well, I'm hoping…"

Feeling the temperature in my face rise to where my skin tone was beet red…

"It will go on some more."

There Marie Collins, as the old saying goes "my heart is on your sleeve".

Meanwhile, the football game did go on without the two simple teenagers on the verge of an awesome level in the game of love. A king and queen, No pawns or other players, is what they are. The two, minding their own. He smells the aroma of her hair, while she turns the other way from him relishing the warmth and security of his arms around her.

The game did end. Home team won of course. Visitors were taken back to their neighborhood with the loss heavily on the dirty shoulder pads that they wore.

"To answer your question Brett from earlier…uh, hmmm, I too wish it will go on more."

Justice Served?

Marie Collins. My life is yours. I walked her home with my hand in hers!!!

CHAPTER 8
"Another perspective"

Another day, another dollar roger Webb thought to himself as he drug his body into the classroom. Some friends ask him all the time:

"How the hell in the world can you stand to teach those puny freaking ingrates that don't listen to you and treat you like a piece of moldy leftover meatloaf?"

His reply most of the time is:

Justice Served?

"Not all of the students are ingrates. Some of those kids still believe in education first and actually learn something. If one does just that... LEARN, I'll be as happy as a bear in the woods taking a s**t."

He'll do it until he can't do it any more. It's his life, teaching that is. Shoot, the man doesn't have a family to go home to. No, he's not gay! He just likes being a bachelor for now. One day there will be a Mrs. Webb. She'll have to be a strong willed and understanding woman to realize that teaching was his first love and will always be his first love.

This is nice to see for a change, perfect attendance in all of my classes today. Whoa…a miracle if it isn't one. Figures as much, Mr. Angelo and ms. Collins are both side by side. How cute!! Ughhhh! Sounds sort of childish "how cute". It is good to see Brett with a smile on his face instead of nothing. Should have been considered a flat sheet of rock on a side of a mountain, not now though. Women can do wondrous things for a guy don't you think?

BRRIINNNGGGGGG!!!! Blasts the warning bell for class to start.

"(Clap, clap, clap) aw right ladies and gentlemen. Have I got a surprise for everyone and I think you'll love it to death!"

A rumbling from an anxious voice from the back of the class:

"Webb's got a bogus pop-quiz, you all watch it's a quiz."

With that the whole class began to groan in synch.

"To your surprise, no it's not a pop quiz!!"

Again, the entire class:

"Aw right Mr. Webb"

"It's an experiment that I did in high school back in the dinosaur ages that you would benefit from…"

Not a peep from the peanut gallery.

"All of you will be paired off into two's. Otherwise know as (da-da daaaaaa!!!) husbands and wives!!"

Nada, zilch, nil. I can hear a fictional cricket that's chirping in the so silent atmosphere. Then that anonymous voice spoke again…

"How long has this experiment got to go on, cause this is royally insane. Stupid. Plus it stinks!!"

Rumble goes my peanut gallery. I figured that would be coming. Hey, for all the grief they give me throughout the school year, have to get back at them somehow. On the other hand, it will teach them something. What, haven't got a single clue!! The exercise will teach each student something different. Hopefully it will be good. Now the fun begins, the pairing off of the happy couples. Ha-ha-ha!! Can I be totally obscene in this procedure or what? Sure I can!! The teacher can do anything when it comes to an assignment (within school curricular guidelines). Then it began. One by one, pair by pair. Some couples were opposites of their beloved, and then other weren't.

"Kim and john are couple number nine, last but not least, Brett and Marie are our lovely couple number ten."

Peaking up from the list of couples towards number 10, that match-up was an unselfish move. How did I know that that certain couple would *be a good one? Ancient Chinese secret.*

Little do students know what teachers do behind their backs. Sure Mr. Webb did think that Brett and Marie would be an excellent pair, but what they didn't know was dear teacher Mr. Webb was reading their journals!! Who could miss how these two kids look at each other during class, only a blind person! Nothing towards the seeing impaired mind you. Young love makes any person feel fresh and happy every single second of the day. Guess that leaves out the old man huh?

Once the list was done, the peanut gallery started again to basically bitch among themselves. Sheer torment is so fulfilling to watch. Sounds sadistic huh. These kids expect us adults to bend over and kiss their backsides, give into their whims and whines. Not me!! Teach them is what I'm here to for and is what I'll do. They are our future. If this world doesn't guide these children correctly now, the days to come aren't going to be anything to look forward to!!

Other teachers around in the teachers lounge ask me if I'm afraid of what the kids are capable of doing. Guns, metal pipes, homemade type knives made in their parent's garages are the types of things being snuck into class. Parents awhile back at a P.T.A. meeting suggested metal detectors to be used on students, as they would walk in the doors. "Asinine" as my response to that fool. Why should we? Some cities, sure. But depending on the amount of crime where you're living. Here, we've never had (knock on wood) that much crime in the school halls besides the typical bully beating up a bookworm while walking home.

Those aren't the only type of crimes going on!! Crimes such as someone blowing away a convenient store clerk for just $26bucks in the register; or a punk druggie robbing an old lady sitting down on a park bench in broad daylight. Not such an ordinary one is an adult grown man getting his jollies, his sickening perverted jollies off of a child. His own damned flesh and blood at that!!! There is no reason in this world why he should do that to him, to anyone for hat fact!! If he's so hard up on sexual release that's what he's got two hands and a bathroom for!! Two resources that are almost found everywhere.

The rules and guidelines were explained to my newly betrothed couples before the bell saved them. It only lasts for two weeks. They don't realize I could've made it for a whole month! peace and quiet at last. No papers to sign or grade for that matter. Time for a nice cool frosty one. Cant help it, I've always been a "head" man. Ever since college come to think of it. Never could quite hold down hard liquor, just beer. Grabbing my jacket and gathering what went into my briefcase, I went around the classroom to make sure there were no surprises left ther over the weekend.

About a month or so ago, I was doing the same thing.getting ready to leave for the weekend. I did enjoy the two day hiatus then. As I was sipping on a hot cup of java that certain Monday morning did I notice the nose grabbing aroma. GREAT!! The

Justice Served?

idiotic janitor forgot to empty the trash again. He did empty it. AGGGHHHHHH!!! It stank to high heaven in here. Maybe it'll go away if the windows were opened and a breeze got going in the room. First period started to file into the room. Then it happened. Half way through class, a student yelled:

"Mr. Webb, some freaking moron fool stuffed a tuna fish sandwich in the book closet..." displaying the evidence in the air as it dripped onto the floor below. Smelled like a woman...well you know. Made my nose hairs curl up. Sickening!! Delicious as it might have been at one time, a starving dog wouldn't have even eaten this.

S.M. Allfrey

So I now check all the cabinets and desks before I leave. No tuna sandwiches. Here I come ohhh frosty one, bye clover high.

CHAPTER 9
"The Little One"

Birthday number 15 has come and gone. Old man didn't do a friggin thing. Mikie did make a homemade card in his art class at school today. Corny, but hey, at least he remembered!!

"Happy birthday Brett"

The card read on the front. He got the "Brett" part spelled right. It's the thought that counts. Mikie, for a little brother, is the best brother that any older brother could wish for. Granted, he does the typical little brother things like following me around and hits me up to play G.I. Joe with him. Hey there isn't any adult doing it for him. A few more years and we're out of here!! That's what I plan at least.

Marie and I have been doing pretty excellent. Holding hand, passing notes in English under Webb's nose, and an occasional make out session on the back porch of my house. At night when the old man is away fro his weekend of sleaze, best time to play sort of speak. "Petting" is the farthest we go. That's what I read it's called in a book about sex education. One of those nights it almost went further, but believe it or not, I didn't feel comfortable. Laugh if you will. The macho male felt scared. Uh-huh.

Feeling like my old man is what petrified me!!

Puzzled and dumbfounded, Marie began to button up her shirt and asked me in a puffy breath…

"You (hu-huh huhhh) stopped… why? (Huh-huh-huhh) I mean if you don't f-f-f-find me pretty…"

"NO!!!! Marie, don't you dare even thing that!! You know that I love you!! There's nothing in the world…I just cant explain it…I don't want to hurt you!!"

cry. Crying is the next thing I did cause that poor son-of-a-bitch alcoholic, shit eating grin bastard of a father is inadvertently robbing me of an awesome feeling. Because of what he took from me four years ago, I can't get the nerve to go on with my life. The urge, the desire just to be "loved" by someone else, is down the friggin porcelain god. The chance, the opportunity to get near a wonderful girl is gone out from underneath me like that cheap trick where two bit magician pulls a table cloth out from under a table full of dishes. The result of this "trick" is a shattered mess!! Dishes, no, but of my heart! What am I supposed to do now? WHAT??

"Better go in now Marie, mikie's got to go to bed. You going to be okay getting home?"

"Yeah, I'll be fine. I'm not mad Brett okay really I'm not. Luvs and kisses to you."

And made that kissing motion with her hand to me. Off she went into the wild blue yonder.

No, you're not mad, but I sure the hell am!! Mad as a tick on a dogs behind. Sucking that sweet nectar

Justice Served?

(blood) for food. Smashing his face in would feel REAL relieving right now. Then I went inside to put the little one to bed.

All the lights were off in the house except for the lamp light inside by the front door. Old man had to have some sort of light so he wouldn't stumble and smash anything after coming home. Did it really matter? He usually staggers and falls smack on his butt anyways.

The little one wasn't in his room like normal. Wondering where he could be, I started to search the house. First was my room. He likes to go in there to read my spider man comic books. Nope, he's not in there either. Next was the old man's room. He wouldn't go in there either cause the old man threatened both us boys early on that if we ever went in his room our butts would be out on the street in some dirty alley to live. Humph! Loving thing to say to kids. All the rooms were checked. Wait a second. There's another room, the attic. How could he get up there? This time of year it gets cold up there cause of a crack in the window, thanks to a no-longer-friend-of-mine 's bee-bee gun. Old man never found out. CREEEAAKKK. SCCREEECHHH, the hinges screamed as I pulled the door down. Something or someone was surely up there.

"Mikie, you up there?????"

Zero sound. A mousetrap went off though. Poor mouse being decapitated for a piece of cheese. Our mousetraps weren't the kind that would just go snap. And would leave the mouse dazed. Nah!! Old man

Justice Served?

insisted on getting top of the line "killer traps". Spring on these suckers had a razor sharp edge where it came down after they'd snap. Pop goes the weasel. Pop goes the mouse's head in this story.

SHOOT!! Getting a cool breeze from up there, Almost good as an ice cold shower. Junior's even decided to wake up for awhile.

"Come on Mikie, if you're up there let me know so I'd know where to look. You going to end up with a cold don't want that now do you?"

Forget this, I'm closing this stupid friggin door.

If you feel any connection between you and your brother, you wont close that door!!! Look harder for him Brett, do it now for gods sake!!!

"B-b-Brett…"

Whispers out from a shadowy corner of the attic walls.

The fear of the unknown made me even more curious, and my feet went toward the corner from where the sound came from.

All huddled up, sobbing his eye out behind some boxes was mikie. Similar to as if some bad guy took his candy away, he looked straight into my eyes with his and let out a wail that would last for approximately 15 minutes.

During the process of him soaking my shirt, I got him down out of the attic, how, I still don't know to this day, into his room, wiped his cheeks and yes dry with my shirt sleeve. He wouldn't calm down. He kept on rocking back and forth, back and forth…sobbing.

Justice Served?

"What happened mikie? Did you do a no-no? You didn't try and cook on the stove again did you? The house want burned down, so that answered my own question. Come on mikie, it couldn't have been that bad what ever it was!!! You aren't hurt are you?? No blood on you anywhere, so you're fine. Mikie, calm down please okay. Let's get ready for bed."

Are you ready for what's about to take place?? Think so huh…

He normally likes to wear his Bugs Bunny pajamas, so I rummaged through his dresser drawer and found them. I went to go help him with his shirt off, but turned around and found him in a fetal position on his bed clutching his private area.

NOOOOOOO!!!!!!!!!!!!! Nothing was in my mind. Blank. Mikie…not him. What has happened? What has that *sorry bastard done? In my mind I already knew though! To my total disgust, I knew. He's doing exactly the same thing I did and still do, after the old man is done. Yes, I know, but the old man swore up and down that he wouldn't go near my little brother if I continued on with him. In my naïve mind, it was the only solution to keep the little one safe, a bargaining chip if you will. A kid like Mikie, ANY kid for that fact should NEVER have to go through with any type of abuse. NEVER!!!!! It's the icing on the cake. The old man promised!! Believing that he'd keep his word made me feel that I should keep up my end of the bargain. It was the only way!! Deals off old man, you've screwed with the wrong one this time!!*

Justice Served?

"Dear journal:

The time has come. Where am I going to get the nerve to carry it through?? Got to get it somewhere. It should have never happened to mikie. NEVER!! When he least expects it, that's for sure. How would he like it to be hurt like he's hurt us?? Like he's still hurting me? Not much that's for sure. I'll make sure of that. Don't have that much money so we could get away. I've got to figure out a way that's all cause the little one is counting on me. As far as the old man goes, that's going to take awhile."

My journal has been in most aspects, been my best friend. It doesn't talk back, give me grief, it listens to me unconditionally, and that's all. These last few years have been in most part, all for nothing.

When I thought I was shielding mikie from him, the man was making his move. Gross, mind boggling, and stomach churning.

I was through with my "friend" and decided to go check on the little one.

The little one was in a so familiar uneasy way; sound asleep…in a fetal position.

CHAPTER 10
"Aftertaste"

    Unfortunately mikie didn't sleep that well last night. All he did was toss and turn, back and forth. Miserable kid has to go through hell like that. He couldn't fend off the old man being the size he is. You compare an adult male, approximately 5'8" or so and about 200lbs in weight, mikie was a toy in comparison! He'd be a toy to play with when ever he pleased. Revolting!!!

So much was racing around in mikie's mind right now; he could have been racing the Indy 500. Why was the key question. Why would daddy do anything (to him) that's so strange? It's "out of character" if you will. Mommies and daddies do THAT, not him. There was a time that he heard a funny noise in their room and thought daddy was hurting mommy, so he went in there to see if she was okay. They were just fine. The little one had no idea in the world what they were doing. They knew what they were doing, at the least the old man did. Mommy was normally so drunk and out of it, her body was there in bed, but her mind was with her lover…the bottle.

A black hole is what the kid will go into. Mikie knows what happened but doesn't clearly and fully understand it yet. It will pull him further and further into a humongous like oversized pair of vice grips that keep their strong hold on him that are Cold to the touch and hard as a piece of uncut diamond with determination to never let go of him.

He's not going to be able to stand this much longer. What he didn't tell Brett was that this whole thing has been going on longer than he thought. It first started a year or so back. Daddy would wait till the middle of the night. Mikie didn't know what time because he couldn't tell time yet. It was always so cold and dark in his room without a light. The old man wouldn't allow him to have any sort of night-light. Brett bought him a kiddie night light last year for his birthday, and the old man threw it smack in the trashcan like nothing mattered. A light doesn't serve any purpose in the realm of deceit. See, if a light of any sort shone in the little one's room, the world wouldn't know what goes on in the Angelo household. And the old man wouldn't have that happen. This house was his playground of sorts. He had his "favorite toys" to take pleasure in. That's what the old man thought his sons were, toys. He made them and he could break them!! Brett (the main course) would always be first; the little one (desert) would be last. He would Hippity-hoppity from bed to bed like a bunny rabbit in mating season. Makes you want to tie the man down on a bed of REAL SHARP NAILS and wave an unwaxed cucumber in front of his nose and tell him what you're going to do with it and see how he really likes it!! As demented and twisted as he's been, he'd probably enjoy the whole thing.

A normal parent wouldn't do this to their kin. Experiences like these ruins a persons mind for the rest of their lives. Childhood is supposed to be girls and boys playing at playgrounds in the sandboxes with one another. The girls want to bake sand pies and the boys want to build skyscrapers that will reach the sky. Fathers throw ball in front yard with their sons, mothers show the daughters what the difference between sugar and salt is when they're cooking. Reality comes knocking on your door as hard as crooked vacuum salesperson. BAM! BAM! BAM! Endless, irritating noise that causes your toes to curl up.

Situations like this one, unfortunately, run rampant in this society. Society does not know how to handle it. Most are blind to the plague that has taken over. It will leave a bland nasty foul smelling taste in your mouth if you leave it there. What would you do about the problem, take care of it??? How is a kids supposed to do that? How are they supposed to get rid of the aftertaste?

CHAPTER 11
"Summertime job"

Taking my own advice from my "friend", that summer after turning 15, I went to go find a job. I had to after what I found out about the little one. That situation had to be put on hold somehow. For the time being, Mikie came to sleep with me in my room. We're better in a pair. The old man was thrown for a loop not knowing why all of a sudden why Mikie came to sleep in my room. I said that it was a kiddie phase that he was going through and that he'd be over it in a couple of weeks or so. Poor baby cant play anymore. Makes me want to cry. Awwwww, touch s**t!

Where could I find a job? Not having a single inkling on where to look, I rode my bike down the local corner convenient store and bought a newspaper. It didn't take me long at all, ten minutes or so at the max. The old man wasn't home so I could scope the classifieds without him finding out what my plan to do was. Page after page, endless descriptions of waitress jobs to nightshift janitors at an office building. I'm too young for those jobs. Here we go, good old fast food restaurants. Stereotyped as a burger slinger. Fabulous!! If it will bring us (Mikie and I) closer to hitting the road, it will have to do for now.

Justice Served?

Monday morning after the old man left for work, I took Mikie over to me-maw's house for her to watch him. She knew what I was trying to do and swore that she wouldn't ell a soul. Me-maw always kept HER word. I had nothing to worry about. My first interview was at 10a.m. at Mickie's (we all know that one). In the ad in the paper, it said that they were hiring of the morning and mid-day shifts, applicants would have to be at least 15yrs of age. That's me! There's probably not a lot that they'll let me do, but what they give me, I'll do gladly. Sweeping the floors, stocking the shelves, whatever it takes. I'll do anything for the little one.

It went terrific. Miss Mills (my NOW employer) the manager was the one that did the interview. She did the interviews for the 15-16 year olds.

Plus she was the one on shift. The process of the interview itself was nerve raking to the highest. My palms were all sweaty, I had dry mouth that tasted like a piece of sandpaper, and my eyes kept on falling down to her bosoms. I read that in the dictionary after I called one of my teacher's anatomy parts by the word "tits". It's what my old called them, so I just assumed that was the correct word. Anyways...ms mills "bosom" were kind of playing hide and seek with the buttons on her shirt. Keep your mind out of the gutter and back on the questions. Boobs aren't as important than getting some cashola and fleeing the clutches of the old man.

The job was just as I thought it would be. There were certain things I couldn't do because of my age like using certain pieces of equipment and going in the walk in freezer. It may sound stupid, but when ms. Mills explained to me why I couldn't do any of that, it made all the sense in the world. I had to wait until the next week to start because my uniform had to be ordered from their main office supplier. In two weeks time or so is when I get my first paycheck. I'm going to have to buy some shoes for work on that one. How am I going to hide those shoes from the old man? He can't find out that I have a job. Ms. Mills showed me that they have employee lockers in the break room that I could put them in. What I didn't ell was the real reason why I needed to hide them. I told her that I didn't want to get them dirty on the way home. She bought it. As far as my uniform went, I'll figure something out later.

To my surprise when I got home, the old man was already there. It wasn't even noon yet and he was home. What's the deal?

The beast hasn't been fed in awhile; he wanted to be fed now!!!

"Boy where in tarnation have you been?? And where the hell is your little brother?? Speak up boy!!"

Now what? Had to think of something and something quick.

"Mikie's over at me-maw's house cause I had to go to school and pre-register for school next year."

He didn't say anything. Absolute silence. Then…

"Bout time you got off your lazy butt and did something. Go get me a brewski boy…NOW!!"

What the devil did I have to do for this man to be at least proud of me??? This man couldn't be proud of

Justice Served?

me even if I just won the Nobel Peace prize for global peace. I'll get you your friggin beer all right old man, and give you what you deserve. The fridge was stocked with his stinky booze. I grabbed a can out, shook it up as hard as I could without letting it explode on me and walked into the living room.

"Well, you going to stand there like a jackass or give me my damned beer?"

It couldn't be that easy!!

"WELL, I'M WAITING!"

He asked for it. I practically shoved the beer into his lap and tried to leave the room as fast as I could without showing him that I was running. FIVE. FOUR. THREE. TWO. ONE…blast off!!

"AWWWWWWWWW!!!"

shook the windows as my little surprise made its entrance. Hilarious if you ask me. The old man didn't think so. Needless to say I made my self-scarce after that. I had to vent a tiny bit. He-he-he.

Mikie and me-maw were making chocolate chip brownies when I walked in the back porches' door.

"Brett, look at whut I dun. I 'elpin me-maw wit da cookeeezz. Wahnt wun?"

"Sounds pretty good guy. We're going to have to go home now, daddy's home."

He knew what that meant. We had to go home and NOW. Mikie gave me-maw a kiss goodbye and told her that he'd be back soon.

Rain began to fall down half way around the block. Darn!! If I felt that it was going to rain, I would have *brought a slicker for Mikie. My immune system is a strong one, his isn't. He could get sick and stay that way for weeks. Something else I also forgot was the laundry. Oh no. I should be able to take care of it in between reading comics with the little one and fetching the old man's beer. Can't forget to do my work uniform. Whites in one load, jeans in another, and dark clothes in the other. For a kid my age, I do laundry pretty dang good.*

Morning shift promptly started at 8a.m. Ms. Mills did my orientation of the area I did today. Every few weeks you change areas so you'll know how to do most everything after while. She took me into the employee break room and sat me down in front of the t.v. to watch yet another wonderful video. This is going to be so much fun.

"Now Brett, I'm going to have you watch these station videos on how to work your new station properly and then you just put the next one in when the other is finished.

Off she went into the world of French fries and burgers.

All in all the training went well. Watching videos for about three hours, but hey. Ms. Mills told me that the on the job training would start as a crew trainer, so I was to go home and a get a good nights sleep. Good night's sleep isn't easy to come by in the Angelo household. That didn't need to be known to everyone else.

Second day on this station and so far so good. James, the crew trainer, first reviewed what I watched yesterday on the videos. He then

Justice Served?

gave me a tour of the entire area. Not that I would be spending my time there. The worst area I think was the garbage area. It smelled as if a dead carcass was buried there or something. Well, you figure that food that's been sitting in that gigantic metal "can" for a week, it'll begin to smell before long. It had the flies and cats trying to eat their way through the door to the trash. Nausea will settle in your stomach if a person stands there too long. On that note, we both went back inside where it was safe from flesh eating insects.

This is really interesting. My most favorite station, the French-fry station. Granted it got extremely hot at the fry's cause of the grease and heat lamps, but I liked it anyways. Somehow my mind got side tracked back to when I found out about what was going on with Mikie. Absently I then dropped a basket of fries down in the vat to cook. Gazing at the fries while they were cooking, "dancing and jumping in the boiling hot oil. Makes me wish that the old man's head were that basket of potatoes. Watching him suffer as the 360* oil covered his head, the skin peeling back as it's pulling off his face from his cheekbones. The irreversible damage that can never be fixed with any type of help. All the layers of skin barbecued pitch black and crispy. This is a frying station or is it not?? He never took pity in our cries of pleading so why should I listen to his now????

"The timers going off Brett, you have to take them out no longer than 10 seconds after the timer goes off or they will burn crisp! Hellllllloooooo"

(A woman's voice was saying so softly.)

This is totally insane. Falling sleep at the wheel sort of speaking is not good for my male ego.

"I'm okay ms. Mills, guess it might be the heat that I'm not used to. Can I go get something to drink before I do faint?"

"Sure sweetheart, go ahead. Don't need anything happing to our new employee now do we? Matter of fact, why don't you go ahead and take your scheduled break since your going to be here until one. Since you're a minor, you have to take a 35 min brake okay. Go ahead and grab something to eat while you're at it, might make your stomach feel better too."

I do have a dollar in my pocket, just enough for a cheeseburger at least.

Gosh, ms. Mills is nice. Bet she's that way with all the employees!! Almost like a mother figure.

Working isn't as bad as I thought it would be. The old man makes it seem like it's similar to sitting down in a dentist chair and having a root canal performed without any medicine. Over exaggeration to the hilt. When I picked the little one up from me-maws and we were walking home, I handed him something in a bag from work.

"Gee Brett, whuts dis?"

Like a kid on Christmas morning, he ripped into the wrapping as if it didn't matter in the world. The present was revealed…

".dis iz neetoooeee, uh weetle Joe tingie. Tanks Brett!"

As he hopped in my arms to give me a hug. All it was was a kiddie toy meal from work. It's what I could

Justice Served?

afford at the moment. Mikie needs a treat once in while. This job's going to work out before too long, and then Mikie and I can get on to the road to freedom.

CHAPTER 12
"Truth"

    It being my day off from work, I thought that Mikie and I would go to the park or something so he could play with other kids his own age for a bit. Putting on a shirt that has a picture of some basketball playing dude on it, I zipped up my jeans, tied my shoes (that was crusted with a nice layer of hardened mud), and went to go see if the little one was up from bed yet. That's stupid. He's up *before the sun even decides to stretch its long gorgeous colorful beams of heaven.*

Telepathically, Mikie knew that I was going to do something with him today because he was already ready like I presumed. Mikie, in a round about way, is getting his independence or a personality of his own. Dressing him was already taking care of for he did it himself. Successfully matching his blue and green colored shorts, which had a rip in the hem from where he tried to climb our fence in the backyard and didn't succeed. His tank top shirt that was a shade lighter then the kitchen curtains, almost like baby puke. Anyways, out the door we went.

Our street was dead silent this time of morning. Husbands weren't home yet from their all night poker games, sons were trying to recover from the study session over their friend's house that was really a drinking game called "colonel puff-puff". Ninety nine percent of them lost. Then there was the wonderful example of a father figure, the old man, in which was nowhere in sight to be found. No loss to me or anyone for that fact. Sweat began to drip into my eye and I wiped it with my shirt. Stung a bit but went away after I swiped it gone. Every time I thought about the old man or got near him in the same room, sweat would begin to run out of my pores like a raging river. Stop thinking about it!! Our street (which was named after our first president, Washington) was at an end and we made a brisk turn to the left for the park.

Justice Served?

Technically speaking the park itself is about a mile or so from the house. Neither one of us minds the walk. We get to people watch on the way, takes up most of the time while we stroll along sanders Ave. Sanders Ave was other wise known as the snobby part of this town cause of all the hoity toity people that live there. These folks gave us some good people watching material. On the left hand side of us, a rather tall, muscular built man was mowing his lawn in a pastel pink colored alligator shirt, other wise known as the preppie shirt back then, khaki shorts that came to his knees, and deck shoes on his freshly pedicured feet. He was so worried of getting his clothes soiled, that he had to stop and wipe himself off. If you're going to be doing something like yard work. Don't be a jackass and wear your friggin best "attire". Shove the alligator!!

To your right of us ladies and gentlemen, this is a doozie!! Ms "I'm too good for manual labor and get my pampered skin dirty" was sitting on a lounger type chair with an umbrella attached to the back of it, was watching her housekeeper wash and wax her convertible!! Oh this is so exhausting for her to sit there while the housekeeper is getting blisters on her hands trying to wax the car to the perfect shine for her highness. They're the kind that after a time of rubbing them, the blood and puss will begin to run down your arm and sting like hell cause the raw meat of the open wound is being expose to pressure that it shouldn't be exposed to. For a second there the woman

Justice Served?

kept on going before she gave up because of it being too painful.

"Ms...I'm..." threw a royal hissie when the poor woman went inside to tend to her hands. The car had to be done before her date tonight. La-te-dah. Housekeeper was thinking:

"Screw you miss debutant!!"

Nice soap opera in the land of rich people.

"yooo Brett, we here"

He yelled out to me so anxiously as we at last reached the fence of Cooper Park.

All in all cooper park is a nice park for the little kids. Right when you get inside the fence an obstacle course starts that goes around the whole edge of the grounds and ends back right here. Few steps on in is the tube slides that will shock you as you're sliding down cause of all the *static in the air. Mikie usually plays in the sandboxes. He pretends that he builds a house for the two of us and the old man cant move in. This house protects us from the old man. Weird huh? Mikie should be building castles and forts of kinds pretending he's in a far away land with Martians or something like that. He's got the right idea though!! I like to sit on the bench next to the sandboxes and just watch him for hours if I could. Puts you in another world for a while.*

Off to the north side a bit of the park was Lincoln cemetery. Most cemeteries you'd think that they'd be eerie and spooky to look at, but not this one. It's actually beautiful to gaze at. Guess cause of the background of it. Sarah Lincoln, back in the 1800's was one of the most beautiful women in the town. The smartest too, cause

Justice Served?

she was educated. Everyone, including the men respected her. Until one day when some villains decided to try and make toast out of the town and ravage all the women. Sarah Lincoln stood up for the town; all towns' people were in awe of her courage. She lost thought and was raped and killed by the villains, that's how the cemetery got its name. Cemeteries are typecasted as a spooky, eerie, place where unresolved souls have the freedom to roam in the darkness of night. You think if you walk in there that a hand will break the surface of a freshly dug grave and pull you back k down into the coffin and keep you for company eternally. The nails of your host encrusted with soil to the point where the embalming solution was ever so sluggishly dripping from where use to be a hang nail that the mortician forgot to take care of. No way in hell am I walking in that place with the chance of becoming worm food!! But for some reason my thoughts stayed with it until we were ready to leave.

It was almost to the point where we wouldn't be able to see the way home without a flashlight and we began to go home. Mikie ended up with the whole sandbox in his shoes and had a hard time walking home, so he stopped for a second outside the wrought iron fence of the cemetery. Coincidence? Maybe not. Puzzled on the decision of taking Mikie in there or waiting another day and go when he's not with me, I asked:

"Mikie, want to go in there for a minute?"

Looking back down to him. He had the sand all dumped out of his shoes

Justice Served?

into two piles all neat by the wall, and was tying his laces back up so he wouldn't trip and fall on his face.

"Huh? Yewww wanna go in der? Naw way Jose!!"

He answered so strongly. Guess that was it on that subject. Another time for sure!! And on we went down to Snob Street.

Oh stinking wonderful, the truck is in the driveway. That makes my day. I was thinking that he'd be gone until we got home from the park, now I'll have to go through the third degree on where we were. How harmful can going to the park be? Not very, but the old man wanted us home when HE got home just to have us in his controlling clutches. Clutches that are so strong that he still has ME in them. There's not a thing that I could do about it, and that's the way I've felt for years. If I do anything remotely going against the old man, he'll destroy the plan faster than a cat can crap over waxed linoleum floor.

Walking inside the front and we were greeted by the sound of:

"About friggin time you lazy on good ass got home, go and get me a beer boy, I'm thirsty. An' don't go and shake the bastard up either!!"

He knew that I did that. I was lucky as a four-leaf clover that my backside wasn't black and blue from a good tannin. The old man doesn't believe in that sort of punishment. He enjoyed other sorts of physical and mental torture. I went and got the beer, unshaken of course, and placed it on the end table next to the old man's permanent place setting, which was the couch. He proceeded to drag himself upstairs to bed later on. A question popped in my mind and I absolutely had to ask the old man something.

"Dad (that's what I called him to his face) do you know anyone in Lincoln?"

Nothing. Not a word. The old man couldn't answer a simple question. Only thing that mattered any to him was his liquid nourishment. There was an absent quizzical kind of look on his face though almost like as if he didn't care for the question that was being asked. He began to sit up in the couch to a position that was defensive. Now what did I do? He's got that look like he's going to pounce me like a piece of beef getting tenderized crazy with a wooden meat mallet. He started to head to rock back and forth in the motion as if saying "yep, uh huh." then he answered:

"Sure do boy. They've been there for a couple of years now. There wasn't no funeral or nuttin'. Deserves all they got…"

As if on cure he turns his head to me and finishes what he began…

"She's in a paupers grave in a cheap ass pine box!!"

How cold hearted can any person get about someone else's death? Talks about them as if they were a dirty piece of laundry that's lying on the bedroom floor waiting in a lifeless heap for cleaning day. WAIT…HE SAID "SHE"!!! That couldn't be. He wouldn't be so stupid as to slip up and give me a clue to where "she" is! I've got to go and check this out now before it eats at me like termites to wood for lunch.

Justice Served?

"Come on Mikie, we got to go back to the park, you forgot you jacket…come on NOW!"

We were out the front door before he could take another sip from his dinner. This is completely out of this world. Why would he say anything to me about "her" like that? "She" can't be. It was kind of weird how it happened.

Tiny beads of salty sweat began to fall from my forehead and into my eyes by the time we got to Sanders Street. No more preppie's trying to do their lawn. By the time we reached the park fence, the beads turned to buckets pouring out of my skin. Finally, we were at the wrought iron fence of Lincoln cemetery. A paupers grave, what do they look like? All I see around is those types of headstones that look like they costs a years worth of rent, all fancy and ornate type you know. They're above ground too, not the one that goes into the soil and are flat to the appearance. Through the front gates we went with a horrendously sounding screeeeeechhhing of the hinges rubbing against each other as the rust that accumulated began to flake off bit-by-bit, layer-by-layer.

There was a locator directory right when you walk in the gate for the graves so when grieving family members couldn't find the gravesite of their beloved all they had to do was know the number of the plot and WHAMO! They could find them. In this friggin case I had no dang idea what I was looking for. There was two side of this so-called directory, and then I found what I was looking for. The words were all faded cause of the sun always shining on them but all that was legible was: rows are by the tens. The ones without names are located in the back of "pauper" section, and the ones with names are in the front. The old man would not be so bold!! Or would he?

Row by row, name by name. They weren't in alphabetical order. Guess that's what happens when you don't prepare yourself for the inevitable future. One of them was a baby girl: born Sept 12, 1991-died Sept 25, 1991. Parents were probably so out of whack with their little baby just passing away; they didn't have any idea what to logically do with her. Sad. Another DID HAVE a name on it. Pete "street" Wilson died: 1978. Sounded like a homeless man that didn't have a soul in the world to care the slightest for him, so after dying while inhaling some cheap liquor, a city social worker did was to order a plain pine box, and even buried him in the clothes that he died in because "they didn't want to be bothered" with people like that. Old dirty, smelling, hole pants; pants that had stains of urine in the crotch area cause he missed his intended target (which was normally a bush); and shoes that were two sizes too small for him but he wore them anyway cause some lady gave them to him. Little did the social worker know that his future held the same fate as of the homeless man.

What's the old saying? What goes around, comes around…

I shook my head in disgust. No one deserves to be remembered like that, well maybe just one the old man. Oh well, to the next marker. Only a number. Number after number. It goes on for rows. Some I passed up and then some I gazed down on quickly to see if anything would catch my eye. Mikie started to get real restless and began to fiddle with the flowers that were left on some of the markers. Guess I better head on home before too long. Not even realizing I was stepping on some markers, I kind of cringed thinking the people in the graves are yelling at me to get the hell off their beds and them in peace. Then I looked down. There it was:

"Sarah Angelo died 1989"

With my eyes plastered wide open as if being propped with toothpicks. Ironic and a twist of fate having the same name as the cemetery. I couldn't breath normal, my heart was beating erratically, and I plopped down on the ground like a sack of potatoes. A rush of tears started to well up in the corner of my eyes. The little one galloped over to me and asked:

"What up Brett...deeeed yew hurt yourself??"

He didn't have to know for I was sitting on the evidence. By this time my shirt collar was totally soaked by the flood of tears. Why didn't he tell me that momma died? How could he do this to mikie, leaving him with no momma for these past few years? It has been so damned difficult to try and be both parents to him. Old man didn't know what he went through with crying at night thinking a boogieman was sin his closet waiting to get him. Better yet, the time that when he busted his chin up so bad I thought he was going to have to go to the emergency room for stitches. No way did he know cause the man didn't exist in our lives. He has his world and we had ours. I slowly got up from momma's marker, pushing Mikie out of the way before he could see what was written on it.

"Come on guy, we're going to get in trouble if we don't get home okay. Come on now."

Huffing and puffing trying to shield him from the pain of discovering what I just did.

To what lengths will the old man go to hurt me? Pretty extreme if you ask me. One thing for sure that I know, the old man WILL NOT LIVE THIS DOWN!!

Lincoln cemetery was now behind us, heartache and all.

"Momma, your death will not be in vain", played in my mind like a broken

S.M. Allfrey

record as we both trailed our way home.

CHAPTER 13

School begins in about there weeks, but that was the furthest thing on my mind. Momma deserves more than a simple flat piece of metal immortalizing her like a four-legged animal that got in the way of a huge truck on the highway. Some how I've got to move her to the regular section if that's possible. And without the old man knowing about it!! Mikie never has found out.

My intentions about the moving were well intended, but stopped. The man at the cemetery explained to me because of my age, and without a legal guardian over the age of 18, I couldn't have her moved without a court order. He asked me if I could have a parent that would sign the request form, I told him no. That scraps that plan. If I went to the court system, the old man would easily find out what my intentions were. That would bring him too much satisfaction indeed.

The "death man" neatly took the papers in his hands and folded them up into the right hand side of his desk in the "out" file. I call him that cause he was wearing one of those black pin stripped polyester suits that was stiffer than a piece of cardboard; shoes that looked like he's had them since the seventies; and the worst…raggedy looking rug on his head that resembled a dead cat on the side of the street. Makes you want to take a nice and hard wooden bat and slug the daylights out of it to make sure it's dead. Almost like as if the poor thing was moving, it started to wiggle Or better yet, like when a cat curls up on a chair patiently waiting for it's owner to pet him.

He thanked me for visiting the Lincoln cemetery office and ushered me out the door, and he didn't let it hit me on the a** well you know. How courteous of him.

Some way, some how, momma has got to be moved. I need to at least get a proper headstone for her. Granted she was a drunk all the time she was with us, but that don't mean cow-chips…she still is a human being. Actually I should say WAS. I was once more drawn to the plot where she rested. No flowers, no burial wreath or anything. Bare to the bone sort of speak. With all my hatred towards the old man, I couldn't even cover up something like this to a family member. The old man was one of a kind when it came to feelings though. He could be standing down in the depths of Hades with the devil himself and he'd think it's a club med or something. Sitting Indian style down on the ground now, my legs fell asleep and the feeling started to crawl up my left side up to my rib cage. I have got to get up before this kills me. And then…

"You think you bad ass now huh boy?"

a husky love voice asked me. It was the old man.

Justice Served?

Nothing in the world prepared me for this moment. Confrontation is inevitable now. Sure, I could try and run for it, but sooner or later he'd get me. This is an event that has been in his mouth like stale aftertaste of his beer, flat, dry, and cruel. Ever since we went to the lake that one summer and we came home to his telling us that momma just up and flew the coop. Nah, he's been itching to do this for years!! Man to man, mono to mono.

"Didn't think you'd figger it out this soon. Aw hell, you haven't got the brains to do much else than to pick your ugly nose. Do you eat them too? Probably do huh? Thought so boy. Cant got your tongue or something boy? Got anything worth saying to me boy, come on now, you've been waiting' to, so do it you weakling excuse for a son."

What could I say? Insults, him degrading me like that and all I could do was absolute zero. Motionless, still, stone like, or better yet, statuesque. Expressionless. No smile to see just hard to touch, cold to the feel. That's what the old man has turned me into, his pawn to move as he pleases, and a light switch that he could flip on or off when he felt the need. This switch is about to get a permanent short in it!!!

"Wh-y-y-y didn't y-y-y-you tell me t-t-that momma dies and that she didn't run off on Mikie and me?"

That's it. That was the big tongue lashing of the century. I was STILL under the old man's spell. Weak if you ask me. If I really told him how I felt, I'd end up picking my teeth off the

Justice Served?

ground. I at last got up from the ground and brushed off the blades of grass that innocently stuck to the seat of my pants.

Come on now, you can do it Brett!!!

Bringing my right arm out with a clenched fist ready to fight the old man, and getting my balance on the ground below my feet, the fist started towards the old man's gut. At least that's what was going on in my head!! There is no way that I could get back at the old man without any repercussions against mikie and I. Speaking of the old man, he was in front of me still with that sarcastic grin on his face when he knows t here's been a defeat on my half. One of these days old man, I'm going to wipe that grin right off that sick, disgusting face of yours and I'll enjoy doing it just

S.M. Allfrey

like you've been enjoying what you've been doing for years to your sons!!

CHAPTER 14
"His plan"

The developments of the last couple weeks have made up my mind for me. Something has got to be done about the old man, and it has to be done soon!! When he found me at Lincoln cemetery on top of momma's grave, I thought I was going to die! He then threatened me that if I told anyone else about finding where she was, cause everyone in the neighborhood AND the family thinks *that she ran away to a mental health place to get her act together, that he'd kill me and Mikie. He would "come" to us in the night and then kill us both in front of each other slowly by torturing first the little one. It would be done that way so I'd have to watch. After I was gone and couldn't protect the little one, he'd have the time of his life. Made the milk in my stomach curdle to the point of making me feel like I have to puke. Determination. That is what I'm going to have to have going up against the old man. Believe you me, after all the mental and physical undoing that he's put Mikie and I through the last few years, if it takes every single breath and amount of energy that I have left in my body and soul, the mouse will be caught!! Sweet justice will be tasted in the mouth of this victim.*

Justice Served?

So many things have to be thought of to make it happen smoothly. Make what happen?? My god, what the hells fire am I thinking of?? What I've been pondering since the first time he came in my bed, but not until NOW did I understand what I was thinking. And end to it all. Yeah that's it. But what if it takes me in the process?? That a chance I'm going to have to take. Nothing matters to me anymore. I thought Marie would help some of the pain go away from my every day routine, but he found out about her too!! He's got to take all that has ever mattered anything to me from me. I can't take this anymore!!!! How am I going to tell Marie that it's off?, Or That I can no longer see her? She's going to be curious as to the reason of the break up. Marie's not a stupid broad as the old man put it when he found out. We're supposed to sneak out to the park tonight, guess I'll have to tell her then.

Part two of Ch. 14

Stars were sparkling as if they were fireworks that kept on going. Bright and shiny to the sight of them. Almost lit up the entire ebony sky. Marie said that she'd meet me around 8o'clock. This entire thing makes me nervous to where my palms are beginning to sweat buckets again. Whenever I get nervous or anxious, it comes out in buckets. The crickets in the bush next to me are starting to chirp softly, it sounds to me like they are chirping. Oh well. Here she comes down the pathway from the fence. I was sitting on a bench near the same sandbox that the little one *was building our house in. Ironic that she's wearing that same blue jean mini-skirt that she was wearing the first time we went out. A farewell memory? This is going to be difficult. Marie sat down next to me and kissed me lightly on the right cheek.*

"I can't stay long, my sister is covering for me cause my parents think I'm locked in my room studying for finals, so what's up babe?"

Was her nickname for me. Hearing her say that to me, knowing what I have to do to her, made me cringe in my underwear with guilt. Got to cut to the chase here and make it quick.

"Marie, babydoll, we aren't going to be able to see each other anymore..." (think of some reason now why Brett) "my daddy says that we're spending too much time together and it's making my grades slip real bad."

Her response startled me completely.

"That's sort of funny...my parents are saying the same thing, that's why I had to sneak out of the house. My guidance counselor called them yesterday telling them if I don't get good marks on the finals this year that he'll keep me back a grade. Isn't that complete bull!!"

Quickly grabbing a hold of my hand. I responded by gently squeezing hers back. Not knowing what to say next, or if I should say anything at all, my eyes went upward towards the stars. The shiny silvery stars. Another system, another world away form this one. Heartbreak is a void that's in ones life caused by being in the wrong place at the wrong time. Weird huh? I finally broke the silence of the stars:

Justice Served?

"Marie, I don't think this whole relationship was a mistake or anything, if anything at all, it taught me how to love another person. The feeling that you've shown me is one that I'll never forget."

Marie was crying her baby browns by this time now. Do I blame her? No I don't. All this pain caused by being unfortunate in the game of love. On my half, the old man is forcing me to not see her no more, and on her half, her parents want her to get good education. Her parents are right for feeling that for their daughter. The old man can run in front of a city bus and have all his insides be splattered all over the pavement for his reason.

That was it. There was the "last kiss" you see in the movies at the end when the hero has to leave the heroine, and she went her way as I went mine. Those baby browns are something I'll quite not forget ever. They'll haunt me for the rest of my life.

Part three of Ch. 14

All sorts of things were running through my mind like New York's rush hour. So many ways that I could get even with the old man makes you think, how could a person so young want to hurt another human for being so bad. What causes them to think of way to hurt them? It could turn out to be a really good topic for a talk show. A good one for sally or Geraldo. The way Geraldo does his show is awesome. I watched him one day when I was playing hookie from school and he had a show about kids that were in their parent's cars when

Justice Served?

the cars were being car-jacked. Punks up there on stage made it seem like no big deal about a kid being in the car that they were trying to steal. Their momma's probably dropped them on their heads when they were babies.

Any person that's been through the same stuff that I have will understand my way of thinking. Maybe not all, but a good portion of them will. Some of them, given the chance, would even help me with what I want to do. It's got to make the bastard suffer like he's made Mikie and I suffer. That poor kid will more likely have to go to a shrink the rest of his life, that's if he don't try and commit suicide first. The thought has crosses my mind many times. You know, the sleeping pills version, the jumping off the ledge of a building version, and diving into a river off a bridge. None of them will take place. If anyone is to die, it's the old man. When he least expects it, and in the most inconspicuous place that he would think and where he'd would be most vulnerable. Guess it's time to go fishing…hmmmmm.

CHAPTER 15
"Another summer"

The end of this school year is something that I myself am not looking forward to. Other students are having end of the year parties and shaving cream runs all around the campus, which is driving every one of the teachers bezerk trying to get to their cars unscathed from the shower of menthol foam. One of the "creamers" instead of using shaving cream, used tat other stuff that takes *the hair off of women's legs and armpits. Their victims didn't know what it was until they went home and began to wash the shaving cream out of their hair. Screams were heard all over town for miles. Now, the principal said that he'd suspend anyone that was found with anything remotely looking like a shaving cream or hair remover can. They got sneaked in when no one was looking. Breaking up with Marie a few weeks back didn't help the party atmosphere either. I don't care about the end of this year or the beginning of the next one. The old man took care of that for me speaking of the devil. It being the end of the school year and beginning of summer vacation, we all know what that means. The lake. This plan of mine might even be easier than I had thought. I hope the old man doesn't think anything suspicious. It's the only way that I could think to take care of the problem.*

Part two of Ch. 15

Old man had us get everything together a bit sooner then usual. I had all the sleeping bags and the cooler that he almost dropped that one-year, but couldn't find our backpacks for the clothes. They got to be around here somewhere. Actually they could be classified as duffle bags because they're so big. The old had us use those cause he was too lazy to wash clothes while we were at the lake. There was one of those wash-a-teria's right next to the office, but he had us cram those backpacks to the gills with all of our shirts, pants and such. One summer I ran out of clean underwear and he made me wash them out by the spigot next to the cabin. Talk about some raunchy, stiff smelling draws. That last word is drawn out to sound like a southern accent. Anyways, He was might anxious to get to the lake this year.

It was hotter then a steam bath this summer. Especially being near the water, it made it stuffier and more humid then usual. GREAT!! My draws are going to get used up even quicker this time, the cotton material gathering at the waistband, bunching up in the crease of my butt. Sticking to my skin with the stench of day old body sweat. Whew!!! No crease bunches. Better scrounge up a bucket or something to wash them in; I'm not going to rinse them out like that one time. Old man has been staring at me for some time now. Saying nothing, just glaring. He's up to something; I feel it when I look back at him. By this time, we made it back up to the normal stomping grounds for the summer and all was unpacked from the truck. Mikie by the edge of the water trying to catch the tadpoles that have made a home out of the footprint in the muddy edge that filled up with water. Slimy sperm shaped bodies flapping all over the footprint. It's beginning to get dark now and I haven't even started to think of supper yet. The old man is going to get upset before too long if he doesn't have anything resembling food to shove down his ugly mug of a face. Stew sounds easy enough for me. Pop the lid, plop it in the pan over the fire, and 1-2-3, food! The brown gravy starts to bubble and throws the aroma of simmering potatoes and chunks of beef around the campsite. Heads pop out of the tents and door of cabins open to the curiosity of what is teasing their noses. No complaints from the little one, he eats whatever I fix. He might as well have licked the plate clean. Either that or just call him rover. It's darker now and the crickets are out. The time is getting closer.

When it comes to coming to the lake, the old man is too predictable. By the time for Mikie's bedtime, he was already up at the office trying to get this summer's clerk to go in the bushes with him for a five minute "tab". If she's smart, she'll turn him down in a New York minute. Me, I read out on the porch of the cabin until the mosquitoes bug me enough that I cant stand being out there and then go to bed.

Horror books have always caught my eye for some reason, so I read a good nerve tingling book by the genius the "king" and this book is about vampires that take over a town, and I'm at the part when these people are trying to kill the "head" vampire. Heyyyy! I recognize that smell. Right in an instant I close my eyes, inhale a few breaths, and remember where I did smell that before. Meetings in the park, snuggling in my back yard until she was late, that's MARIE!!!

What was she doing here??? Folding my book so I wouldn't loose my place, putting it down on my lap, and deciding should I or shouldn't I look up. It's only your imagination; she wouldn't come to this lake. Now you're going psycho; nutty; or just *plain old crazy. But the aroma pulled my eyes upward to her to see that those brown pools of loveliness staring but yet inviting me to take a plunge in. Lilacs, that's what that smell is, Sweet and relaxing which overpowers the weak. Stuttering came out of my lips:*

"Y-y-you-r-re here? What? I...uh... uh, I..."

Once more those pools said come, and she said:

"I'll go if you want me to."

"NOOO!! I don't...(starting to laugh) I don't know what to say. It's a surprise to see you that's all, a GOOD ONE don't get me wrong."

Stupid idiot, now she thinks you're completely weird. Ask her if she would like to sit with you. She won't do that after what happened.

"Can I come up?" (Motioning to the seat next to him)

Getting up to greet her like a gentleman should do, the "king's" book fell to the boards of the porch. That's almost like desecrating a shrine or something holy. Hey, I like his books okay. Wiping the book off and putting it inside on my bed, I came back out and offered her the chair next to where I was sitting. Questions started to surface almost like how oil comes up from the ground, in gushes.

"So, you come up here all the time?"

"Naw, not a lot. My parents thought I would be good for me to get out of the city and into some fresh air for a couple of days. I'm bored already and we haven't even been here but

since about noon. When did you get here?"

"Sometime around between four or five. My dad is up at the office and my little brother is in bed fast asleep."

"Want to still sit outside for a bit?"

"Sure I do, with you, anytime."

She looked at me funny, but didn't say a word. You could tell she knew that I broke up with her for a different reason than what I gave her. Not a peep. We sat there until the old man saw us then she ran off to her cabin. He did it again, damn him!! This sounds like an old cliché, but I lost her once and no way in gods green earth will I let him take her away from me again…over my dead body!

Justice Served?

Part three of Ch. 15

That was the last straw!! Just because he thinks he can control me for the rest of my life, he will not and I mean NOT EVER TAKE HER AWAY FROM ME AGAIN! The temperature in my cheeks began to rise for they were turning beet red with disgust and total hatred for this man. I love Marie too much, that I shouldn't even have let her go the first time. The old man, how could one person be an exact definition of evil? At least in my mind he is. He comes up to me on the porch and stands there right in front of me. RIGHT NOW!! RIGHT HERE, I COULD END IT ALL. But how, How could a teenage boy like me, go up against a huge, indestructible being like the old man? There's always a loophole of some kind to get around thing like that. The one certain definition that sticks out in my mind of evil is this one:

Evil: anything that which produces pain, calamity, etc…

That should be changed to:

Evil: the old man.

Simple, but yet to the point.

Stale smell of the beer that he must have been drinking up on his little rendezvous with the clerk once again leaked from the cracks in between his teeth and just kept on coming. He was doing something that's for sue cause while looking down away from his gaze, I saw that his fly was half zipped up and part of his shirt was playing hide and seek. Aw man, the clerk was dumb enough to fall for his plea. I wonder what story he told her. If she's smart enough, she'll cut his "tab" off right now. She won't see him *no more. He got what he wanted, even if it was for just five minutes.*

The motion for me to come inside was made, and I followed after him. One more time, that's it. I can't take it anymore!! If I go through with this I'll explode like a tire that's been mistakenly left hooked up to an air hose. KAABOOOM!! Pieces strewn all to kingdom come with no chance of being put back together, floating, gliding down to settle on the hard cold reality of what is about to happen.

Mikie was long gone and fast asleep on his side of the wall (which was actually a sheet from momma's bed)

Dividing our room from the old mans, I unsteadily treaded to his cot. I sat down with the echo of springs yelling out a loud squeeeeakk beneath me as the weight of the old man followed behind.

I should know better by now shouldn't I? That's difficult to say unless you've been there. It's different for everyone that this has happened to. Not all have the thoughts that I'm having, all the things that I'm planning for that fact. Who in their right mind would? I just can't even think straight right now. Fifteen years old and I still let him do it. He wont be prepared for it. He won't see it coming. Where am I going to get the strength or even the nerve to put up with it much longer? Don't know, but somewhere it will come forth.

For what seemed like an eternity, we both say there on the sacrificial alter. Him coursing out his every move, me on the dream of getting out of this nightmare and then it began.

Justice Served?

My upper torso portion of my body was strongly forced down on the mattress as my legs were left dangling off the edge. The shirt that covered my chest now lay down on the floor after being peeled off as if to torture me more then he has too. Yeah that's what he considered it all right, it was his delight and my torture! Button by button being undone and the springs were yelling now even more but were muffled by the weight of our bodies. His was already off and his dark smelling body hair that covered him practically from head to toe, pressed against my barren creamed colored chest. My desperate pleas for help weren't answered as he continued on with the sickening event.

Those helpless pleas made on and on while his chubby calloused fingers traced their way down to my belt buckle and undid it. An order for me to take my jeans off was made, and I obeyed. The heat of the summer night mixed in with the body heat gave me the feeling once more of throwing up. That always happens. It never goes away. It stays there. The sacrificer quickly stopped me from making the attempt of getting up as he flipped me over and shoved my face down into the mattress almost to the point of where one of the springs couldn't make another sound. I brought my hands up to the frame and wrapped them around it to keep me from doing something too soon, too early. My knuckles turned white, but not yet Brett, NOT QUITE YET! Pain flushed in my veins as if it were blood itself. No longer…

Justice Served?

I released my left hand from the sweaty death like grip, paused for a second pondering what I was about to do. More then anything in this world, me, myself...I wanted to go on. Finger by finger, my hand slid underneath the soaked mattress and met the touch of cold steel.

As quick as lightening striking a pole on top of a building in the middle of a midsummer's storm, that hidden cold steel was introduced to the old man in a way of a kitchen carving knife. He was for once surprised. Squirming out from underneath him, I shoved the four-inch blade in even deeper into his chest, right where it should be. In the heart! Now this to me was a long time over due pleasure. The old man tried to push me away, but didn't succeed, the blade started to sever the wall of the heart. Muscular as the heart is, I made the knife go further by twisting it back and forth, which had caused the warm thick liquid river of blood to turn into a geyser. Drops spewed into the fold my mouth and I wiped them away with my other free hand. The old man was now lying still as a statue on his altar intended for ME. NO MORE IN MY LIFETIME WILL HE TAKE ADVANTAGE OF ME AGAIN!! The blood was everywhere, painting the wall if you will with the strokes of his death. Spreading out over the wooden logs that the cabin was made of. Mikie…oohhh damn! What if the old man woke him up? Then what is to happen? I had to make sure he was not able to get up ever again, and bringing the already soaked bladed knife up in the darkness of the cabin, striking his hardened heart for

Justice Served?

the last time This time not pulling it out so quickly as I did the first time. For some reason the blade had no trouble at all slicing into the bastard's battery of life. After all, if the heart doesn't pump the blood, you don't live…PERIOD! Unless, you're fortunate enough to be near a hospital that could hook you up to machines for the rest of your life. Gee whiz, isn't that hilarious old man? No hospital to help you now. No hospital for you like there was no one for mikie or me when you were molesting us in our own house. Like I've already said earlier, he will not do anything to us ever again. The blade innocently fell from my grip with a thud landing right by my feet. Poking around the curtain I see that the little one is undisturbed and dozing like a lamb. Good!! Now to dispose of the garbage.

I put my pants and shirt back on, couldn't find my draws though anywhere. Then began to try and drag the large lump of lifeless human being out of the cabin. He's too big. His dead weight is too much for me to handle by myself there's got to be a way to get him out of here with out bringing any attention to me or to the cabin. The little one will be fine asleep, curled up in a tiny snoring sounding ball in his sleeping bag. It's his most favorite thing in the world cause it's his number one bunny on the front of it holding a carrot. There has to be a way to get the old man out of here.

His stout frame was lying there, still as the night outside the door. No sound came from his lips, not a breath from his lungs. By this time the blood had begun to get crusted

Justice Served?

around the entrance of the first wound, but the fresh one still had some blood sort of sitting on top of the wound. Anytime I had expected the sorry human being to get up and beat the living crap out of me and make me pay for standing up to him. Not this time. Here's a real morbid tidbit. Right now at the position he's in, he'd make a real good edition to a horror wax museum.

How could a fifteen-year-old boy be so cold and callous about just taking a life of another human being? My thought about that is when you're in my shoes even for a minute, you'd understand how I feel at this moment. If you at the age of then (the earliest I can remember) were having something you didn't comprehend or understand why YOU being done to you, after all the years it would build up to the point where you could no longer stand it. The point where you NOW understood what was happening to you is what would throw you over the edge. That's when you would do something about it.

Does that mean particularly, you'd go out and find the largest gun or knife to go and blow the aggressor to smithereens or chop them up into small pieces and feed them to the animals? No. Does that make it right to commit such a fiendish act in the feeling of revenge, No it doesn't. See, the act of any sort of violence, no matter what it is, isn't for everyone. Especially when the act is Murder! But for me it is, and it was. It gave me the release that I've longed for and that I've needed for years just from the knowing that he wouldn't harm or come anywhere near me or the little one anymore. The rush is similar to getting a small buzz off of a six-pack of cheap beer. I close my eyes for what it seemed a long time, to enjoy the sensation of the victory over the old man. Before too long, his big old heifer body will get stiff and harder than a rock, so I've got to get him out. I've already tried to get him out though. Cant bring no one else into this charade, don't want to chance it. The old man always carries odds and end things in the back of the truck, so he must have some type of rope or towing chain. THAT'S IT.I'LL DRAG HIM.

After checking another time on Mikie, I go out into the night, reminiscing what I've just done, and go to see if the old man had such things in the truck. Sure enough, he did. It was one of those bright yellow towing ropes with the silver metal hooks on the end to connect underneath the disabled vehicle. This will work perfect. Nice and touch enough to drag his happy ass into a ravine somewhere, where I could put his body into and sink it so it wouldn't be found for weeks. The rush isn't quite gone yet. The feeling is almost gone.

Doing that, now I had to worry about the rest. Coincidently enough, there was sort of a small pond about a mile or so from our cabin. Beavers pond is what it should be called, cause of the water in the pond was there due to a dam built by a couple of busy beavers that didn't even pay attention to me as I put his body slowly into the water and watched it sink further down into the depths. The air from his body started to come up in bubbles. There, they are almost gone now. He wont be found, not for a while. By that time, I'll be back home with Mikie and will say he went on one of his floozie finding weekends and didn't come back. Me-maw will attest to that. I will never be suspected. The only ones that will know about this are my best friend, the devil, and myself. Speaking of my best friend, I haven't written to it in a long time. It's got to know what has happened. One of the beavers poked their head up, stopping to stare at me as if it knew what I just did, mocking me like saying "it may be your friend now, but it wont be later..." Crazy animal.

"Dear journal..."

CHAPTER 16
"Alibi"

    It took me a good part of the night to clean up my mess because by the time I got back from the disposal process, the blood soaked into the wooden logs real good. They were fairly smooth type logs, so it wouldn't be that difficult to lighten up the stains by a nice long scrubbing. The sun began to poke its head over the horizon, when at last the final spot was scoured. Not all of the "maroon" *color was totally gone, but the spot looked like the knots that you'd find in wood anyways so they blended in to my advantage. Mikie was turning around in his sleeping bag and trying to wake up but ended up on turning right back over and continued to snore some more. Thank god!! I got to get this nasty bucket full of water and dump it somewhere before all the other campers start to get up.*

The water, by this time, had this revolting, irony smell to it like as if it were drawn from a country well and not from a cities water supply where all the impure stuff was taken out and fluoride put in, brownish and smelly. Makes me loose my appetite now. It's the other way around believe it or not; I could eat a horse. Probably all that scrubbing throughout the night that added to the exhaustion. My entire body was aching to the point where I was so stiff that my fingers couldn't even move they were so sore. The whole things is done and over with. No more neglect, no more mental abuse, and finally…no more visits in the middle of the night by the old man. Most people like and enjoy visits by their family members. They'd be glad that they didn't get THESE TYPE.

Birds and all sorts of animals were waking up when I was disposing of the irony contents in the bucket. I found a barren patch of dead bushes approximately ten or so yards from the side of the cabin and tossed it with a heave. Splash it went and covered the ground around the lifeless plants. The bushes were dead anyways, so it didn't matter if I threw it there or not. Life would never

Justice Served?

come back to them. What was ironic in a way was that the soil sucked all of it; every tiny miniscule drop of what it thought was life. That water to that bush was like the blood was to the old man's heart. Non-existent now.

We'll stay here for the rest of the day. I'll tell Mikie that the old man took off and he'll think that he went on one of his infamous binges of booze and women. Mikie likes to play in the edge of the water of the lake in the mornings. Me, I couldn't do anything for what it seemed like forever but only ended up to be about an hour. Sitting there, where the night before, Marie and I sat together. Looking at the early risers get ready for their busy days ahead of either fishing to their hearts content, or hiking into the woods and getting lost. Guys named Jim-bob are the imbicles wearing the neon colored wadding boots in the middle of the lake. Then bimbos named Buffy are the ones that get lost in the woods because they didn't follow the trail signs. They didn't think they had to follow them I guess. They'll do what ever they want to do!! Serves them right. No need to worry, the whole campground is like a national park, it's surrounded by fences and makeshift lean-tos incase there are people that think they don't have to follow the rules.

Not even realizing that the little one got up, he zoomed past me (already fully dressed) headed in the direction of the lake. That made me basically fall off the chair and onto the porch. Dusting the dirt off the backside of my pants and making a cloud as the dust settled downward, a sheet of welcomed heaviness took over my eyes and I plopped back into the chair. Sleep, this feels good. Dreams. What type of dreams would I have now since the old man is no longer here? Fabulous ones that's what type. Fear free. Sounds like a sick advertising campaign. A person has to have some peace and quiet ever now and then. Now it's my turn.

I wonder what he's doing right now she's tossing around in her mind. She's wondering if she should go and see if he would want to go for a walk or hike in the woods. Cant do that. He'll think I'm being too pushy or aggressive. It felt like she was going to open up to me last night though until her father barged into the picture. Fat slob is what he is. I really shouldn't talk about someone else's parents like that, but the man is down right creepy!! From the way he walks, to the way he stares a person down. What he did last night was uncool. If I had a daughter that was old enough to date, he's the type of "thing" that I'd want to keep away from her. He belongs in a pig's pen he's so revolting. Marie closed her lovely browns and pictured her and Brett in a kiss on his back porch of his house. A crystal clear drop of saliva gathered and began to drop from her mouth. Oh my goodness, I'm drooling, as a rabid dog would be while having rabies. Cant help the feeling though. Brett brings out the most in me. Hey, don't want to sound like the school hussy now. All right! she makes me as horny as an only female rabbit in a cage full of male ones! Horny as a toad, there I said it. I'll go and try to see if he wants to speak to me, after I get dressed of course.

Justice Served?

She got together a one piece hot pink colored bathing suit and matching shorts with a pair of year old flip flops that were falling apart on the bottoms. It was summer and she was at the lake. It wasn't like she was here to impress any certain male friend. Only if she knew hat he was going to be here, her mini-skirt would have come in the suitcase too!! Out the cabin door she went. Marie was off in the direction of her sweet young beau.

Marie crept around a tree that stood in front of Brett's cabin trying to see if the old man was anywhere to be seen. She didn't want to have to run away from him again. He was down right creepy to the bone. Excellent, he was nowhere in sight. But where is Brett?? Aww, there he is on the front porch, taking a snooze in the same exact chair that he was sitting in the night before. This is so cute. He's all still, with his hands folded almost looking like he was lying in a coffin waiting to be buried in a grave.

"AAGHHHHHHHHHHHHH!!"

She went as the "sleeping beauty" moved. Brett was so startled from the scream that he bolted up and ended up landing on his butt quicker then he did when Mikie flew out this morning.

"What the heck was that???"

Brett got up with such grace and poise that he landed right back on his backside. Noticing that he landed in an unnatural position, his eyes opened wide and wider when he realized what that spot was. He must not have done a good job of cleaning up the garbage last night. A dime sized kidney shaped drop of blood was there in broad daylight for *everyone to see and gawk at. This is friggin terrific. There has to be totally and completely no evidence of what went on here last night or I'll spend the rest of my life in a place where huge burly guys will fight over me as a cellmate. They like to call the new guys "boy toys". If any of the other prisoners came near you they wouldn't live to see daylight. Young virgin meant is what they chanted as I entered the cellblock. It gives me goose pimples all over my entire body thinking about it. To tell you the truth, it probably wouldn't be much different from what the old man did. Sad to say that huh, but Things like that happens in today's world. Unfortunately for the victims that is. Marie didn't notice what I was trying to hide, so I acted like I was finishing* dusting off my pants…for the third time today.

This was a change for the better, the both of us speaking to each other again. After that abrupt "dear john" that the old man forced me to do, I figured that she wouldn't want to have the slightest thing to do with me. Teenage love, easily repairable you idiot, ask her to sit down or something.

"Well, you going to stand there and laugh at me or you going to come up here and sit down?"

We both started to laugh hysterically until our eyes teared up and our sides began to hurt. During our break down, Marie did come up on the porch and did sit down. She couldn't seem to stop giggling even after she sat down and had some time to calm down. Her laughter

Justice Served?

turned quickly into a muffled chuckle as she tried to cover her mouth so none of the campers could hear what a food she must have sounded like. Oh well, who cares. I sure didn't as long as she was right next to me!! This outfit she was wearing didn't help my.um.shall I say friend "junior" at the moment. Great! Something that I don't really need at the moment if he decides to rise to the occasion, she's probably going to think that I wanted her to come up here just to jump her bones. Not that the thought didn't cross my mind, but that more then likely would scare her away in a flash. We both sat there, hands in our laps looking at one another, listening to the woods animals wake up from the night before.

Time went by like as if the entire world stood still. The only thing that mattered in the whole universe was Marie and I. All else around us didn't seem to matter much. Reality was about to get cruel and slap me in the face when Mikie came up to the porch steps. Our hands were still in our laps.

"Brett, I gettunnn hungreee. Can I get sum tin' to eat now??"

Mikie looked over to Marie and waved his hand to her as if saying hi. He got kind of shy around any female. Wait till he gets into puberty, he wont know what to think then. Still under Marie's heavenly spell I responded to the little one:

"Sure guy. What do you want? Daddy's not here so we can have what ever we want okay. How about Mac-n-cheese with wieners? Does that sound good to ya?"

Without hesitance, the little one questioned:

"Where deed he go? Is he coming back??"

What was I going to do? This isn't going to work. Someone will find out. No one will find out. There's only one other "person" that knows anything about last night and that's my best friend, my journal. And it's hidden away in a place where no one will ever find it, NO ONE!! Mikie will never know what I had to do last night; he's too fragile to handle anything like that. Even though he's gone through the abuse given to us by the old man, he shouldn't have to learn what it's like to kill someone in cold blood. He deserved an answer of some kind.

"Well, Mikie, I don't think he's coming back for awhile. You see he

even left some money if we need to get anything plus the cabin is paid up for another week."

"Wee can stay here?"

"Yep."

As I shook my head to him, all he could do was to jump up and down with utter joy. He was aware that the old man wasn't going to be there, and that seemed to give him a sense of safety of sorts. That's nice to see from him for once. He continued to jump all around the campground. Looked like he had some Mexican jumping beans in his underwear or something. Marie was staring me right in the face when I turned back around to her.

"What?"

She didn't answer for a minute and then she opened her lips:

"Your dad isn't going to be here? That means you (with a coyish look on her face) will, umm, be all by yourself right?"

Now her eyes were glazed over looking at me once again. Then I realized why she was asking me that. WE CAN BE ALONE!! Only if we wanted to take a walk or sit on the porch and last but not least, neck for hours in the bushes, we will never again be interrupted by the nasty fat s.o.b.

"Breeeettttt, I'm hungreeeeee!!"

Snap out of it Brett, you'll have time for that later. Feed the poor kid before he lies on the ground aching from hunger.

I'd better get him something to grub on before he start to howl at the sky. Turning my face to hers:

You want to have lunch with us? Nothing fancy, but it'll fill you up just the same."

The love of my life smack dab in front of me and all I could offer her was Mac-n-cheese and wieners. Isn't that appetizing? To my surprise and delight, her answer:

"Hey, even if it's only that, as long as it's with you Brett, it will make me the happiest girl in the campsite. Need some help?"

Thrown back by her response, I couldn't answer her right away, the awesome Marie Collins eating lunch with me. It's like she round about giving me another chance after breaking up with her a few months back. Wonder if she's gone out with any other guy? The way she looks and the type of person she is, any guy would be an accomplished and *certified moron not to consider going with her.*

Here's you second chance at life Brett. You'd be a fool not to take it. Especially when it's handed to you on a silver platter! Jobs are given to a person cause they know someone in the company that's a family member: promotions are given to an eager employee that works their butt off from the time they clock in till the time they clock out; but the chance of life?? Only the lucky and the few get that most precious gift. You bet your sweet heart shaped ass Marie Collins, Brett thought to himself. I'm taking this chance as if it were candy to a baby. Sweet and delicious to the taste, that's what it is!!

Part two of ch. 17

Mikie scarfed every single bite of his lunch down as if where his last meal, then headed off to the lake once more. I never have to worry about him drowning or anything like that cause he never actually goes into the water itself. The highest amount of water he goes near only goes up to his ankles. Anything higher than that and he always shies away from it. One time I thought about putting a life jacket on him while he plays, but then realized that it would be pretty stupid and a waist of money if he doesn't use it. Mikie's a pretty smart kid anyways, no worries like that when it comes to him.

Marie and I did go on a walk around the campground. The trail scaled on the outside of the site near the fence *that divided it from the woods themselves. Nice and secluded in some points. Now is the time to tell her precisely why I had to break up with her but to find the right moment in the only problem now. We held one another hands as if attached with crazy glue. Neither of us wanted them to come apart. This felt so right for both of us that we, if this sounds corny, beamed with delight. The path that we were following had twigs strewn all over it and we couldn't help but to step on them as we walked. Snap! Crack!...kept on echoing under the canopy of trees that gave the illusion that another person was following us. The old man!!! He's the only other person that would have the capabilities to pull anything like faking his own death off. Something is behind us and crouching by some brush. It got to the point where all the sounds of the forest were non-existent and all that was heard were the beating of two hearts, mine and Marie's. THUMP-THUMP, THUMP-THUMP, THUMP-THUMP. Branches of a bush started to wiggle and wiggle even more the closer we got to it. Another heart accompanied ours, but this one was a bit quicker as if just being pumped with a syringe full of adrenaline. Without noticing, married tightened her grip on my hand holding on for dear life.*

"What's wrong?"

Asking her as I desperately tried to loosen the vice grip that she had on my defenseless hand.

All she did was to shake her head in the motion as saying "nothings' wrong". She knew what I meant asker her what was wrong, but didn't want to say anything. More branches were moving by this time. This is insane. The old man couldn't be alive. Or could he? Made me want to go hid in the outhouse for the rest of the day. Stupid isn't it? And then...

As if in unison, we both screamed our lungs out and scrambled behind a near by tree. The bush revealed it's temporary inhabitants. I couldn't look out from behind the bark, and Marie had her beautiful head buried in my chest. What if it was the old man coming back for me to make me pay for trying to kill him? He'll hack me up into pieces. No first he'll do what he's been doing for years and then hack me up. Marie will be sitting on the ground too stunned to move, too petrified to help. Come on Brett, be a man. Defend your sweet Marie.

Step by step "it" crept closer and closer to our hiding place. Here it comes, get ready. It it's the last thing you do Brett, you got stand up to him, and I opened my eyes.

"Marie, look."

Not moving from where she was, she softly asked me.

"Do I have to?"

I said to her:

"Yes"

The horrendous and scary thing behind the bush turned out to be an innocent, harmless and hungry rabbit looking for dinner. How idiotic do we feel now? It raised his head up to the both of us and twitched its nose then continued to scurry off into the sunset, sort to say.

Feeling completely stupid and cowardly, I took Marie's hand once more and continued on with our stroll.

She was fine now, a tiny bit shaken from not knowing what the hell it was. But fine other wise. Me on the other hand, it feels like I'll be glancing over my shoulder the rest of my life feeling like the old man's ghost is haunting me.

Part three of ch.17

The sunset had an eerie reddish glow to it today. This is some sort of omen or something?? Thinking to myself. Total malarkey if you ask me. I've got to absolutely cover up last night somehow. Yeah Mr. brightness, how? I have not a clue. Mikie got done with the spaghetti ala tin can stuff that I so graciously fixed for supper tonight, and then off to bed he went. Without asking him too. He's good for doing that. Going back to my previous thoughts, I've got to find an alibi somehow. While picking up the dinner dishes and putting them into the cold water, I didn't want to let them get too crusty like the old man used to let them get. Marie came strolling up the pathway.

"I thought you had to do something with your folks tonight?"

Questioning her with curiosity. Okay, okay, I was prodding.

"Well I sort of fibbed my way out of that. They wanted to play charades of all things can you believe that?"

And she let out a laugh that made her face glow a shade of pink into her cheeks. 'At least you have parents that want to spend time with you even if it is playing a boring game', is what I wanted to say to her, but not wanting to lead her on in any way of to what sort of family life I really had. HAD as in past tense I emphasize.

In that moment, I saw it flash before me. My alibi. There is no possible way that I could put myself to use her as my alibi. She's the only person I can think of at this minute. I can't come out and say: "by the way Marie could you cover for me last night and say I was with you. I went out to the beavers damn and shoved my dead father under the water after plunging a knife into his body countless times. Please with a cherry on top". NO WAY IN THIS LIVING VERSION OF HELL!!

"Is Michael gone down to sleep yet Brett?"

Chuckling under my breath I replied...

"You might not wanna let him hear you say that too loud, he hates to be

called "Michael". He prefers Mikie ever since he could speak. Cute when you think about it. There was a time when he spoke up and said "I'z not Michael, iz name iz Mikie!"

She leaned over towards me and said:

"Then I better not say it again too loud."

Winking at me and planting a huge kiss on my cheek, "what was that for?" asking her bewildered.

"You don't like me kissing you?"

"Oh no! I didn't say that, it's just that when you do that it make me feel all…well."

Junior was saluting her like he was standing in front of the American flag…poised straight up and proud of it. Marie glanced downward and they were inadvertently introduced once again to one another. Now she really *must think I'm a pig! She surprised me by asking:*

"Would you…uhmmm, like to uh.go somewhere where we could be alone?"

ALLRIGHT!! BINGO…

"Marie, I don't want to pressure you into anything that you wouldn't want to happen. I love you and don't want to loose you cause of something like this again…"

Again, a complete turnaround…

"If I don't want to do anything, trust me. I'll let you know. Come on Brett, we got all night."

That night, we made the most awesomely beautiful sweet love that could ever be made. Afraid at the start, I backed off from her, which was a Habit from the old man. He popped into the picture and quickly back out again. HAH!! She's mine and not yours. Caressing her bare warm luscious body, we became one as the night took over the horizon. Feeling as good as I have in years, I made love to her once more and forgot the world on the other side of the cabin door.

Mikie stayed fast asleep on his side of the curtain finally dreaming of good things and not of protecting his body against the old man.

Unknowingly to Brett, his alibi was just made.

CHAPTER 17
"Betrayal"

Summer time come and went for the folks in clover. Nice and quiet, but all the "ears" open for business. Those ears were open as wide as could be when Brett pulled back into town without his daddy as Mikie was on the passenger's side of the truck sucking away on a lollie-pop and Brett in the drivers seat. The most popular story was that the slob of a father off and deserted those poor defenseless kids and left them to fend for themselves. Another good one was that Mr. Angelo (he was always called that, no one knew his first name) went on to the next town over to their local whorehouse, got drunk and couldn't find his way home. Some of the towns gossiping old women live on all the streets that exit from clover, so what comes in and goes out of town, they'll know about it. It's their way of life anymore.

Mrs. Harris, gossiping woman number one, lives on the outskirts of town on Polk Street in a single story adobe style house. Some statues that she has in the front yard are of some amigos wearing sombreros, but staring right at you when you drive by her yard. The further and further you roll away, those eyes seem to follow you. Other then that, she, like any nosey person that wants to know all, has a pair of binoculars by the front window of the house. You cant see the curtains move or tell if there is life inside, but you can feel those lenses burn right into your back as you leave out of town.

The other woman goes by no name. Actually, she's been living in clover for so damned long everyone has forgotten her name. Poor soul is a recluse and don't let anyone inside either. Meals on wheels go to her door quite often, and every once in a while, a grocery deliver service bring her a few bags of groceries to the front door. They don't ring the bell but were instructed to leave them on the front porch. As long as they get paid, who cares what the old hag does. She didn't care a single bit. Like Mrs. Harris, she too had some "looking glasses" t o peer out of on those lonely nights.

Gossiping old woman number one (Mrs. Harris) was quite interested in a faded old green Oldsmobile that Friday afternoon left town. It was riding awfully low to the ground in the back end, so she focused her "eyes" some more to see what was in the front.

Almost every Friday afternoon after work, Jim Fletcher takes off of work about an hour early, packs the trunk of his car with everything that he would need and takes his little boy up to the lake for some father son bonding type of thing. He's also known as the custodian at clover high for the last five or so years.

These trips have happened ever since his wife died some years back by some stupid drunk in a beat up

Justice Served?

pickup truck that side swiped her and left her for the buzzard's sort to say. Hit and run is what the police called it. The boy don't remember much of the incident, he was too young to comprehend what actually took place. So Jim does the best he can with him and taking him to the lake is something that they both like to do. Both him and the boy loves to sit on the edge of the lake and watch the tadpoles jump or try to jump with their not yet developed bodies, in and out of the water. Jim, being a tall and slender man, didn't like the idea of sleeping in a tent. Spiders and snakes, thing like that, is what he didn't like having the chance of creeping uninvited into his sleeping bag in the middle of the night, so he rented a wilderness cabin.

Jim went to go put the sleeping bags into their beds after arriving at the campgrounds, so they'd be ready when his boy got tired. Whoever had the cabin before had arranged the bunk beds to be on one side of the cabin and the single cot on the other. He didn't like them like that, so they were moved to where they were together at the heads of the beds. His boy sometimes would have nightmares of his daddy being taken away from him and would wake up screaming like his head was cut off. Bone rattling shriek is how his neighbors told the cops at two in the morning a couple weeks ago. They understood the situation after Jim explained the root of the nightmare. Jim wanted to be close by in case that happened again.

Justice Served?

While he tried to move the bunks, the edge of the frame (at the foot) drug along the side of the cabin wall and had caught onto something. Being stubborn and hard headed, he tried without looking what the problem was. Over and over like a broken record he tried to move it. Finally his manly pride gave in and went to see what the hold up was. Now this isn't good! There seems to be a crack along the seam of this one log at the base of the floor. Hope there wont be any rain while we're here he thought to himself as he bent down to be at eye level with this troublesome intruder.

Not only is it a pain in the neck, but something else too. Jim fingered around with this crack and discovered that is was some sort of hollowed out hole or hiding place that someone rigged up. For what reason would a person carve out part of a log? This is wild to the extreme. Makes you feel like they're in a mystery movie or something. Let's see what's in there if anything.

Neither Jim nor Brett knew what just took place, Jim being the "founder" of bad news, and Brett (soon) being the receiver of it. From the start of their relationship years ago, Brett thought he only had one good friend that would never deceive him and stand behind him no matter what. That friend would keep all secrets that were told between them like a bond that was as solid as the precious diamond. Is he prepared for this?

Most people don't understand how a bundle of fastened together pieces of paper could be so precious to a person. For some it's more easier to *open up to a diary, journal or whatever you would call it. In his case Brett calls it his best friend. This for him was a release for all of his feelings, his angers, and his sorrows. If he wanted to vent out his frustrations, the opportunity was there. The pages would let him take advantage of them in a way, and not talk back. They were there for him when he needed them. Not once did they slap him on the face, or scream in his ear that he was a worthless little waste of skin. Friends don't do that to one another. This spiral bound notebook that Brett picked up at the grocery store years ago, became priceless to him. Therefore in a sense, became his best friend. What would happen if that trust was broken?*

Jim took out the best friend from the cubbyhole, turned its cover open and began to read from the start. Every detail, all the moment that Brett went through. Brett's only friend, as he put it, was found. The betrayal began.

CHAPTER 18
"Afterward"

By the time Brett and Mikie got home, it was time for the little one to go to bed. Not only did it feel weird for them to pull up to home without the old man, but also it felt so much like a relief. Why? Only the ones that have gone through it will ever understand what that means. After throwing the car keys onto the table by the front door, I walked up to Mikie and asked him if he was even tired at all. His non-challont reply was a casual head nod "yes". I could tell that he was exhausted. He wont have to sleep no more in fear I know that much. Neither will I for that matter.

What is my "best friend" doing now?? It's the best thing that I've ever done. I don't know how I would have been able to stand what I went through for this long without some sort of release. Although it was hard and very destructive at times, my "friend" helped me no matter what condition I was in; it was always there. I'll have to go back up to the cabin in a few weeks and get it. It needs to be destroyed just like my freaking old man was. He's' right where he belongs in the depths of hell where there will be no ice water served!!!!

Justice Served?

Mikie was on the floor again all curled up. I guess it's out of habit. It will take him some time to get used to everything without the old man. Not having to run and hide from the slimeball will be a nice change of pace. I'm not sure how else Mikie is going to handle it. The only thing I can do is to be here for him when he needs it. Taking the blanket off the bed, I covered him up and he seemed to move underneath it just a tad to get comfortable. Letting out a tiny moan as if he were about to wake up, he curled up even more. I turned the lamp out with a slight click and was out of the room for the night. The door was left open just a crack though. I've always done that for him cause I knew he would eventually end up in with me. Remember, it's always better to be two's around the old man.

Beasts seemed to not attack when there were pairs of victims. Less of a chance to get what he wanted. Now the next thing to do would be to get through the next few days and even weeks without any difficulties. The neighborhood "nosey butts" would be the most likely roadblocks sort of speak. Nah, they should be easy to handle. Any sort of juicy gossipy form of story and they'll be like a kid in a candy store, even with their binoculars around their necks.

Since I've been doing it for years, getting Mikie up for school was no problem at all. At least I didn't smack him upside his head if he didn't tie his shoes right! Although later on when I would talk up to the old man and tell him to stop beating on Mikie, he'd take it out on me later that night. I'd rather it happen to me then to the little

Justice Served?

one. All that was in vain though now to have found out about what the old man was doing to the little guy. In vain, not really when the end effects of my actions took care of the matter, that sorry slob deserved what was coming to him and how it happened!! When you come down to it, it was really too good for him. He should have suffered in a much more severe way then what we did, and that's a fact.

Anyways, my mind shouldn't be on that right now. Getting through the next bit of time, just Mikie and I, is all that needs to be on my mind. Breathing in a bit, Brett sat down on the steps waiting while the little one was rummaging in his room trying to find his backpack.

"Brett, where's daddy? It's ok that he's not here. I was just wondering iz all."

I didn't know what to say to him. Inside I was jumping for joy, but yet on the other hand my stomach was in complete chaos. You would think I would feel better about the whole thing, but not me. If I was in the bathroom, I think I'd be tossing my cookies royally. That can't be shown right now in front of the little guy.

"Little man, he's not coming back home. We can get along without him during the meantime like we always have. When momma left us, we did it on our own, so we'll do it again ok bud?" He shook his head to acknowledge what was said and then went right up to bed. The last thing I saw of him was the shadow of his feet against the walls at the top of the

Justice Served?

stairs. A sigh left me, and I too went to bed myself.

CHAPTER 19
"Back To Work"

 Being totally dumbfounded by what he had discovered over his trip with his boy, Jim fumbled w/his key ring on his pant loop and about tore it off but succeeded at last. He sees so much at this school; he's the eyes and ears of this little world. The kids and even the teachers would be amazed and maybe even embarrassed at what he knows. They should call him the keeper of the little people. Wouldn't *that be a hoot? One thing he did know was a way to figure out who's handwriting that was, and when that is done he'll know who did this. You might be asking yourself how in the world does he know to look here. Short and sweet to the point, it's the only school in town and plus this kid (whoever it is) describes it to a tee!! Opening the double doors that was just bolted and locked for the weekend, he went right to his plan.*

Brett already got his brother off and to his class by the time he entered the double doors to his part of the school. Going directly to his locker and not even paying one iota to whatever was around him, he opened his locker. It was a total mess and needed to be cleaned out really bad. His books slammed onto he tiled floor as he dropped them and proceeded to dredge out his disaster. He crumpled up a few of unneeded not turned in homework papers and then shut the locker door. Not wanting to totally shut, he had to use his shoulder to force it to closed. There you go as it finally it gave in. The hallways began to echo loudly w/ the final bell. Man!! The final bell, I'm going to be in deep if I'm late again Brett thought. All the trash and garbage that was already left on the floor by the kids, and it's not even the beginning of first period, blew all over from the children's feet running and trying to not run into each other. Doesn't this make you think of what their rooms at home look like? Jim and his crew were already on the job to sort of speak w/brooms and trashcans in tow. Most of his "crew" took the main part of the halls and he took to the nooks and crannies that *they usually missed underneath the lockers. About half way down he bent down yet again to get some more balled up wads of papers when something made him stop deathly still in his tracks. His fingers proceeded to open it widely while his hands tried not to shake while holding this piece of paper. Checking to make sure he was alone and no one was peering at him for any reason, he then put it back in it's original form that he found it in and shoved it into his pocket. The keys on his custodian key ring made that annoying jingling sound as his hand pushed the paper down into the pocket. Making a mental note of which locker it was found under and moved on. He had to now found out what their name was and then go on from there. Now to go sweet talk the secretary in the front office. Jim loved* to flirt w/the secretary even though she was about twice his age, Sweet older lady but she had some fire in her Jim can vouch for that. If he didn't clean the office like he should (and sometimes he did slack he has to admit) have he would hear it the next day for sure!!! Anyways, he tried to inconspicuously poke his head around the corner of the office to surprise his "girlfriend" but failed miserably. "Alrighty there Jim, whatcha want now?" giggling softly while she turned around away from her keyboard.

"Hey there darling, I need a favor. I found this (pulling out a key ring he's always had in his pocket) this morning while cleaning up and just want to return it before the poor kid thinks he lost it. I know which set of lockers it's about from so all I need is to know the *name and exact locker number and I'll open it with my master key and just put it in before next class lets out." She gave him a lifted up eyebrow and made the comment "now Jim, you know you can't do that without the kids permission. You remember what happened last year don't you w/that one brat of a child blaming us for stealing his radio??" Jim leaned onto the counter and responded right back with: "yeah and as you just said he was a brat trying to make trouble. Come on darling, you know me. I'm just trying to do a good thing here and helping a kid out" she knew he was good people, and she knew darn well he had nothing to do with the radio fiasco last year. Her thing with Jim was that she just liked to "seem" like she was hard ass, but really wasn't. Someone had to keep this school* office in line; it just ended up being her.

"Alright then Jim, hold on a second." Her chair squeaked as she rolled over to the computer that had that information on it. The wheels needed a bad wd- 40 and before she could even ask or open her mouth, Jim beat her to the punch. "Yes, I'll take care of that after I return the key" And winked at her. You wouldn't figure that a woman her age could type as fast as she could, but before you could one, two, three she was surely enough done.

"Brett Angelo, locker number 46..." She swiveled in her chair realizing that she was now talking to herself. "That darn man, I'll never figure him out."

Before the next class was over and the hallways could be invaded by the *ungratefulls, Jim cautiously trailed his steps towards locker number 46. He knew it was in the high school section, which was sort of a relief in the weirdest way knowing what went on in this "discovery" of his over the weekend. It didn't make it though any easier to stomach. What was he going to do after he found out who it was? After he put face w/the handwriting, what was to happen then? He knew what he legally should do, but then on the other hand, no one should get away w/what he or she did. Jim was literally starting to get butterflies in his stomach. A grown man getting nervous about confronting a kid, more and likely a teenager, but still in his mind a kid. Could a kid really be capable of killing someone? He slipped his hand onto the journal that stayed hidden in his other pants pocket (for he wore those huge pocket work pants) then hesitated as he was basically jolted from his boots while the bell rang right over his head. Talk bout making someone want to jump back two feet. He composed himself and went right back into the custodian role and quickly grabbed his broom next to him. The motion of the broom mimicked as if he had a huge pile of dirt, but yet was actually sweeping air. Calm down man he was saying inside his mind, the kid is going to know what's going on if you let him see you being nervous. Jim then gazes upward and looks upon the self appointed executioner of this now deceased man that is somewhere at the bottom of a lake. Brett Angelo…wouldn't have thought. Now the question for Jim to answer is, what to do about it? He had to do the right thing even though he didn't agree w/what the father did, there was a crime that was committed. A situation like this would make anyone go crazy!!!!! I feel for this kid, I really do. All that physical and emotional abuse that from what the journal says, him and his brother went through... UGHHHHHHH!!! Still sweeping air, Jim went back towards his office. The bell rang once again and the halls were empty yet again.*

Part two of ch. 20

Jim just sat there in his chair with his finger on his chin. Thinking from a parents perspective it totally disgusted him what these kids went through. Then on the other hand, taking the law into his own hands like this kid did went racing though his mind. What the hell am I going to do? By no means was he even thinking that he was a perfect person. Killing someone though??? He couldn't do that he doesn't think. Yet, in this kids defense, he don't know what he'd do if he done wrong like these kids. Pulling out the journal from his pocket, he put his right hand on as if to pull some sort of vibe from it. His eyes closed and his hand was still on the cover of the notebook when it literally made him bolt up from his chair. This has to be done, ironically and as sad as it may seem, he had to the right thing. He had to think some more. Something had come to him that he hasn't thought of in quite a while. He was morally twisted. That's why he couldn't make up his mind on what to do. It was totally eating at him like acid would metal. He had to go to church. Yeah, he went to church. Not as often as he should and as often as his wife (when she was living) preferred, but he tried to set good morals and such into his boy. He could go to the police...nah, not yet. Had to think this through some more. The pain and agony of the kids zipped through his mind yet again over and over. Jim left work without even telling his girlfriend at the front office, and raced over to the local church.

Knowing he could talk to the pastor without any confidence being broke, Jim spilled everything. The conversation went on for hours and finally had to be stopped because he had to pick up his son. He was yet reassured again that all confidence would be kept and that he should do what his heart told him to do. Unfortunately, now he knew what he had to do. Jim went to pick up his boy, but before he did that, there was one more stop to make and it would be the hardest he ever had to do.

CHAPTER 20

The sun was almost done shining off the back window into the kitchen as the glare of the rays glistened off the soapsuds from the sink. Mikie loved to try and wash dishes but inadvertently left half them dirty. But, at least he tried. Brett then finished off the kitchen by wiping down the counters, table and such with a hot wet washcloth. He tossed the towel into the sink while standing in the doorway and slowly walked out into *the front porch. Brett felt so free but yet so alone and scared. He did something so terrible, yet his father did too!! The huge and definitive thing was that his father didn't take the law into his hands. His father took other things disgustingly into his own hands. The wicker chair creaked as he settled into it even more but was soon disturbed by a shadow that covered his face. His eyes hesitated from a glare as they opened up and stared right into the sheriff's silver lensed glasses. Not a word came from his mouth as he stood up and straightened his shirt from over his pants.*

"Brett, where's your father?" the lawman asked still motionless to the boy. Not knowing what at all to say or to do, Brett just stood there next to the wicker chair that just moments

Justice Served?

ago helped him ponder the thoughts of what he did. Sadly enough Brett knew what was next to come, but he had only one thing to say to the sheriff.

"Can I call my grandmother to come get my brother? He doesn't know what happened and he really doesn't need to know. She lives right here in town and it wont take long at all." Somberly looking down then back up to the sheriff's silver covered shades.

"Sure Brett, we can do that, here (and he hands me his cell phone) and go ahead and do what has to be done. I'll wait right here. The handcuffs wont even have to be put on in front of him." He knew quite well that it was a much-appreciated gesture on his part, and I then dialed my grandmother's number.

"Grandma, you need to come get mikie for me ok and you have to do it now…" There was no words coming from his mouth as he listened to what was being said on the other end… "Yes grandma, it will be ok, or at least now it will be…Mikie is safe and so am I, but unfortunately I have to go somewhere for a long time and you're the only one I trust him with. Yep, uh huh…I will…" Brett's eyes began to water up and you can tell something now was going on which was very serious…"Yes grandma I did take it into my own hands, I couldn't put up with it anymore. No one really knows what happened in this house. (Crying) please grandma, come pick him up…I'll have his clothes and I'll give you the key so you can come back and get the rest of his stuff ok? Don't forget his blanket ok, he loved

Justice Served?

that blanket…it was the one that mom made him ok." He folds the cell phone closed, wipes his eyes with his other free hand and gives it back to the lawman.

"Thank you for letting me do that sir, he wont understand and probably wont for the longest time."

It took a few minutes for my grandma to get here and by her demeanor and observation of the sheriff standing by me on the front porch, she somberly took the clothes I gathered into a gym bag of mine and went and got Mikie from upstairs. Not wanting to do what came next I faced the inevitable.

Mikie came out the front door w/ grams and looked at me all excited. "Grandma said that was I going to spend the night at her house tonight, is this true Brett?? How come Brett?

Why is this big man w/the funny glass not going away? he looks mean."

"Actually dude…" kneeling down to his level he continued to say "grandma is right. You are going to stay at grandma's house but more likely for more than just tonight ok?" Brett's hands began to shake and tremble and almost began to cry again. Tears did well up into his eyes, but he didn't let it show to his little brother. His grandma finally got the chance to come up to him. Not many words were said; she knew what happened, there was just nothing she could have done that's why she was always there for the boys. It's almost as if she took them as her own children and not just her grandchildren. Mikie would be taken care of well, but her main concern now was with Brett. A boy his age

Justice Served?

doesn't need to be where he's going, and knowing him, he'll own up to what he did and take what's coming. "Lord, help this child and I pray that you'll be welcoming him into open arms once this is over with." She then took Mikie and put him into her car and drove off at what seemed a snails of a pace.

The sheriff finally broke the silence of what seemed like an eternity of standing there looking at the smoke from the tailpipe of grams car.

"Alrighty Brett, you know we got to go now", as he adjusted his shades on his bridge of his nose.

"Yeah I know." And now the tears freely came flowing down his cheeks as if there were no stop to it. But not because of what he did or where he's going, it's because of losing the last of his family due to his actions. His mother, when she was alive, always

tried to instill that in him. His actions can get him into trouble if he doesn't watch it. Not that he was a bad seed or anything when he was younger, just one of them "morals" that she tried to teach both of the kids. Oh well huh…Slam goes the car door and the rest of his life starts.

EPILOGUE

Already donning my new hair doo and my lovely orange ensemble, the ankle cuffs continued to clank as I walked down the infamous last walk. You would think from all what you hear that I'd be nervous and my heart beating faster Nope, not in this case. I knew what was to come now, and honestly I was eerily calm. The only thing that kept me from spazzing or freaking out like I've heard the other convicts do right before hand was to know that my mother was going to be waiting for me. I missed her ever so much. Not enough to do my old man in, but as any kid would miss their mother if they loved her. The point blank thing about the whole thing and when you think about it is that I'm getting the same fate as my old man. I didn't mess around with any little kids though. I didn't beat my wife (not that I'm old enough to even be married) if front of my kids then go take the rest of my anger and disgust out on my sons. All I have to say is that get it over with and just freaking do it!!!!

The guards finally stopped at the solid Plexiglas partition to the chamber and noisily opened it because of the huge hinges on the door. They already ran me through the drill of what would happen and especially what would happen if I "cracked". No worries when it came to that I already said. I held up my wrists to the designated guard that was supposed to unlock them and he did so with so much enthusiasm it brought down the house. That was sarcasm on my part. The guy was just doing his job, but it's not every day that the opportunity is there to put a teenager to death for murdering his father. I think what mainly got the guards after they found out what my "story" was that what the circumstances were that the "deed" took place. The fact that the deceased was molesting his own children and more likely had something to do with the children's mothers death too. On the other hand, as I said before, the guards have a job and as much distaste as they may have, it will be done.

Finally the wrist shackles (?) were removed and as were the legs ones also. I was instructed to go into the next "area" and stand there w/the prison pastor. Not much was said, and as you can tell since before the telling of my "whole story" I'm okay with what is about to take place. I had done it, and now am taking full total responsibility of killing someone. Be it my father or not, it's done and over.

"You know pastor, as corny as it may sound, it's not bothering me at all. They even offered me a Valium to calm my nerves and I refused it. You want to know why pastor?" The pastor shook his head ever so dignified as if he were saying yes. "My mother is going to meet me, did

Justice Served?

you know that? I know a lot of people don't understand that or believe in it, but she'll be there for me. This is quite a change from our talk the other day huh? I know, but I thought about it and came to this...why fight it and why get all worked over something that someone tried to take control of. That's what he was trying to do pastor, take control and finally I had enough. Anyways, just wanted to let you know that and what thoughts have gone through my mind since our meeting. His hand came up onto my shoulder with such warmth anything just left my mind totally.

The next door opened up and we both went into the chamber itself. I turned around knowing well enough that the pastor had to leave and that soon I'd be alone with myself. I was instructed to lie down on top of the table and then the doc came into to administer the IV. Never did I like needles, but hey this time it didn't even hurt! My arms, everything was totally numb to the pain. A few days ago, one of the guards did tell me it's almost like going to sleep, and that most of the death row inmate's cant even tell that the meds are going in because they take the Valium that's offered to them before hand. The tape was being put on the tube of the iv to stay on my arm and all I could think of was how the tape would come off and pull some of my arm hair off...how weird was that huh? I looked around and the curtains to the viewing room weren't open yet. The voice came over the speakers that the execution was about to begin with in the minute. The dark red curtains then opened with ever so much

Justice Served?

anticipation and the two rows of people were sitting there. You could tell some were the press; they loved this sort of thing. Boy did they have a field day. Then you could tell some were the clergy of the town, wanting to witness such an atrocity killing a young child of god. Then you have your people that had a lottery in town of the locals to come witness an execution. You would figure the sicko's would get a kick out of that, but those people you could tell were really taken by this. Especially this homely looking woman with a kerchief in her hand and crying, Go figure. The count down was on and now the red light above the door went on.

The witness gallery was being affected at all, except for the "homely" looking woman. Al l she thought about was her son. She held a *picture in the opposite hand of her now wet kerchief. He had eyes just like the boy on the table. Why was this affecting her so much? She knew why, maybe that's why she turned out with the life she had now…lonely and broken hearted. She should have come forward years ago but she couldn't.*

The switch was thrown, and her son that was gone on the table before her was now also gone in her heart. The picture slowly fell to the prison floor.

ABOUT THE AUTHOR

I am a survivor. Also a wife, friend and mother of three children. This subject matter entered my life as well as I can remember around the age of eight and went on for years. The effects of this went on in the littlest matters and still does to this day. Not to the extreme as it once did, but it is still here with me. One of the hardest things for the victim and even for the offender is that the victim can choose to forgive, but they can't choose whether to forget because it will always be with them. I wrote this for both the offender and offended to let them know how it plagued this writers Life.